"Provides plenty of X-rated thrills and spills, but lodged in this landscape of uniformed desire are little nuggets of genuine human warmth and connection that give the book . . . an emotional charge of a strength and vividness all but unknown in the fancier, more pretentious precincts of same-sex fiction."

—*San Francisco Bay Guardian*

"Putting into service his experiences as an out Marine, and tapping into a network of gay military men with stories to tell, Buchman, the book's editor, has collected candid first-person accounts of hot sexual encounters (including one of his own) with military men from every service branch—from the Army to the Coast Guard. His own on-base sex tale, 'Tank Trail,' concludes the collection with a hot, steamy climax that should satiate anyone who has ever wondered or fantasized about the sexual exploits of gay and gay-curious men in uniform."

—*Unzipped*

"Alex Buchman's keen eye and firsthand knowledge have assembled a collection that is intensely erotic and thought-provoking. Heartily spitting in the eye of porn cliches and expectations, the book stares you down with its hard authenticity and emotional candor. . . . Leaves you excited, confused, and hungry for more. I look forward to future volumes."

—D. Travers Scott
Editor, *Strategic Sex* and *Best Gay Erotica 2000*

"*A Night in the Barracks* confirms all your worst fears about homos in the military. They have sex! Really horny sex. With straight soldiers. The bastards."

—Mark Simpson
Author, *It's a Queer World* and *Saint Morrissey*

"A set of outstanding sexual memoirs, written by current or former servicemen who've had sex with fellow servicemen. . . . *A Night in the Barracks* is a deeper read than the simple stroke book, one that's bound to stay with the reader a long time."

—*Playguy*

NOTES FOR PROFESSIONAL LIBRARIANS AND LIBRARY USERS

This is an original book title published by Harrington Park Press®, an imprint of The Haworth Press, Inc. Unless otherwise noted in specific chapters with attribution, materials in this book have not been previously published elsewhere in any format or language.

CONSERVATION AND PRESERVATION NOTES

All books published by The Haworth Press, Inc. and its imprints are printed on certified pH neutral, acid free book grade paper. This paper meets the minimum requirements of American National Standard for Information Sciences-Permanence of Paper for Printed Material, ANSI Z39.48-1984.

Barracks Bad Boys

Authentic Accounts of Sex in the Armed Forces

HARRINGTON PARK PRESS

Titles of Related Interest

Barrack Buddies and Soldier Lovers: Dialogues with Gay Young Men in the U.S. Military by Steven Zeeland

And the Flag Was Still There: Straight People, Gay People, and Sexuality in the U.S. Military by Lois Shawver

Sailors and Sexual Identity: Crossing the Line Between "Straight" and "Gay" in the U.S. Navy by Steven Zeeland

The Masculine Marine: Homoeroticism in the U.S. Marine Corps by Steven Zeeland

Military Trade by Steven Zeeland

A Night in the Barracks: Authentic Accounts of Sex in the Armed Forces edited by Alex Buchman

Brothers and Others in Arms: The Making of Love and War in Israeli Combat Units by Danny Kaplan

Barracks Bad Boys

Authentic Accounts of Sex in the Armed Forces

Alex Buchman
Editor

Harrington Park Press®
An Imprint of The Haworth Press, Inc.
New York • London • Oxford

Published by

Harrington Park Press®, an imprint of The Haworth Press, Inc., 10 Alice Street, Binghamton, NY 13904-1580.

EDITOR'S NOTE
Depiction or mention of any person in this work should not be construed as an implication of said person's sexual orientation.

Chapter 13, "Navy Daze," is reprinted with permission from the Mark Pinney collection.

Cover design by Jennifer M. Gaska.

Front cover photograph by Steven Zeeland/stevenzeeland.com

Library of Congress Cataloging-in-Publication Data

Barracks bad boys : authentic accounts of sex in the Armed Forces / Alex Buchman, editor.
p. cm.
ISBN 1-56023-367-2 (soft : alk. paper)
1. United States—Armed Forces—Gays—Sexual behavior—Anecdotes. I. Buchman, Alex.

UB418.G38B37 2004
306.76'62—dc22

2003021895

To
Joseph Anton
and
David Clemens

CONTENTS

☆☆

Preface

I want to begin by saying thank you to all the people who made *A Night in the Barracks* such a success.

In my preface to that first volume of *Authentic Accounts of Sex in the Armed Forces* I wrote about my own first attraction to written porn, and the important role it played in helping me come to terms with being gay. I loved the stories with their racy fantasy scenarios. But to my disappointment, I found out that gay sex, especially in the military, was extraordinarily hit-or-miss.

In these *Authentic Accounts* I wanted to reflect the human realities of sex in the military. Some stories are fulfilling and others disappointing. Some are poignant and others embarrassing—even sometimes painful. But most important, all of them are authentic (verified through direct contact with the contributors).

After completing *A Night in the Barracks,* I felt reasonably sure that it was unique, primarily because of its emotional honesty. But I was unsure whether a book of reality military erotica would sell.

I knew from experience that most gay men I met were excited by the prospect of hearing my stories of sex in the Marines. These stories would start out with an almost porn movie set-up, then usually wind up with a (for me) rewarding but not necessarily sexually climactic ending. After hearing several of my accounts, one friend suggested that I should lie and change the endings to make the stories more satisfying. This I found revealing, that many people favor fantasy over reality. This did not allay my hesitations regarding the first anthology.

So I was pleasantly surprised that *A Night in the Barracks* became a gay bookstore best-seller. And I was honored that it garnered excellent reviews, and that one story was even chosen by Susie Bright for *The Best American Erotica 2003* (Simon & Schuster).

A second volume seemed almost inevitable.

I discussed the idea with Steven Zeeland, my esteemed mentor. He proposed that the next anthology focus on military "bad boys."

The topic was definitely not my first choice. This theme fit Steve's new life in the rundown sailor-ridden town of Bremerton, Washington. I meanwhile was adjusting to newly "married" life in Manhattan. Luckily for this book, my beau and/or patience didn't last, so I soon found myself in Seattle again, ready to take on the project.

Then came the events of September 11, 2001. For a time I wasn't sure I could in good conscience continue with this volume. Even if the "bad boys" I had in mind were not exactly the traitorous sort, I felt uncomfortable pursuing an anthology eroticizing military deserters in the post "9/11" climate. So while I took a sabbatical from the project, Steve acted as a clearinghouse for submissions from potential contributors, including Dink Flamingo, Daniel Luckenbill, and Gayle Martin (the latter two being contributors to the first volume).

When I returned to the book, I felt that some of the initial raw material was a little too dark, possibly tainted by the health problems Steve was having at the time. We both began to actively search for some lighter fare to offset the heavier, bleaker stories.

The topic grew on me.

The reasons for doing "bad" things in the military are as varied as those who do them. Sometimes there's not much more to it than youth and inexperience. Not many eighteen-year-olds have a clear picture of what is truly in store for them when they sign their enlistment papers. But the baddest boys here regale us with a certain *cockiness* seemingly unique to the military.

Part of it is being "young, dumb, and full of come"—but even your average frat boy can boast that. A bigger part of it is signing away your life, or what at that age seems like your life, to become a warrior—even if (outside the Marines) most guys who enlist don't obsess about it. Of course there are also plenty of young men (and women) who join the military just to get money for college, or in the hope of serving in some quasi-corporate job. But for some guys enlisting is still a little bit like joining the French Foreign Legion.

As Daniel Luckenbill's story reminds us, there is a long and well-documented history of the U.S. military relying on judges to "sentence" young offenders to enlist. Even after the advent of the "all volunteer" U.S. military of the 1970s, juvenile felons were routinely given the option of jail time or military service. For some, the regimentation and structure of military life proved a blessed stroke of luck, delivering them from poverty, abuse, and a continued life of crime. Others remained criminals, troubled young men whose personal demons no amount of military drill or discipline could exorcize.

A larger question, and one that these stories can only barely begin to address: Is it the "bad boy" who has failed the military or has the military has failed him?

There are many reasons why these stories have the allure that they do. The racy "wrong" feel of the more sensational accounts. The pull on the heartstrings for readers not too jaded to feel for the young servicemen who have good hearts but have gone astray. And the good old American tendency to root for the underdog. . . . Without sin, there is no redemption.

In the most cocky/confident accounts here by civilian pursuers of military men there is an ironic seductive element.

Again and again, an idealized image of military men clashes with a sometimes painful reality.

In "The Trouble with Harry," Gayle Martin confides step by step her relinquishment of control to "a lying, cheating, manipulative piece of shit" Marine (though in the end she gets more than even). In "Trouble Loves Me," Steven Zeeland confesses how his bold flirtation with "neo-physique photography" ends with him falling prey to clean-cut poster image sailors who lock him out of his own studio (though he does have a video to show for it).

Professional pornographer Dink Flamingo's three stories are this book's most fascinating picture of the dynamics of control. One moment Dink is complete master of the situation *and* his AWOL bad boy lover; the next, he's "getting rid of" his roommate for daring to point out that Dink's "guest" has effectively taken control of the household—Dink takes control to maintain his carefully managed surrender of control. (Though in the end . . . Well, there is a reason why Dink gets as much space as he does in this book.)

The first half of *Barracks Bad Boys* has the most hair-raising and heartbreaking stories, but the second half holds the most surprises. Scott Moraz's "What Are Friends For?" is a rarity in erotica—maybe even a first: a straight soldier's detailed account of cheating on his wife to fulfill his virgin gay buddy's obsessive fantasy of sex with the guy he'd been in love with since tenth-grade gym class. In sharp contrast, Steve Kokker's "And the Straight Shall Be Crooked" is a poignant and steamy tale of a gay man "reassuring" a Russian military cadet that his crooked penis need not doom him to celibacy.

Other stories included here have to do with the thrill of danger.

I won't deny that I have pushed some similar boundaries, but I cannot confess to ever having been a true Marine bad boy. I was merely naughty. Mostly I always seemed to be the one to watch over my fellow Marines. Vicarious was always satisfying and safe for me. My secret desire was for events to spin out of control, and then to try to pick up the pieces. My story "Tank Trail" in *A Night in the Barracks* was a rare true example of life imitating porn. My story in this book, "Evil," turns the tables. My initial, and I thought daring, dip into bad boyness turned out to be more than I could stomach.

One last note. The final story in this book, "Navy Daze," turns the tables too. It was found in a cache of vintage porn dating back sixty years and sent from Spain by antiquarian expatriate Mark Pinney. It should be read as a coda. The account was circulated anonymously—illegally—in the 1950s, in mimeograph format. All of the Navy references, period slang, and places mentioned have been verified. There seems to be too much unnecessary detail for it to be just fantasy. Until the ending, which delivers exactly the kind of porn-perfect huge-cocks-ejaculating-simultaneously climax this book is not about.

But, after all, regulations are made to be broken.

So please enjoy *Barracks Bad Boys,* and if you have an authentic (and verifiable) story of your own that might fit a third volume in this series, please send it to me c/o The Haworth Press.

Alex Buchman
March 2004

☆☆

Acknowledgments

Thanks to Alex F, Anissa H, Bill C, Bill P, Dan, Dennis, Diana, Doug, Dwight, Eric, Gabriel, Karl, Kevin, Leland, Mark P, Mark S, Mattilda, Peg, Randy, Rebecca, Steve K, Susie, Trav, and most especially Dave and Joe.

☆1☆ Evil

Alex Buchman

The Humvee lurched into a rut in the dry dirt road, almost throwing two of the four Marines out the back of the truck.

"Watch it!" I yelled at the driver and pounded on the small plastic window on the canvas top of the vehicle. I turned back to the other Marines and we resumed our conversation. It was Rusk's birthday and he was none too happy about spending it in the field.

I was in charge of twenty-five Marines undergoing field training. We had just finished a long hard day of mock infiltrations and equipment testing. This being our fifth day in the field, we were dirty. We were also covered in camo paint, and if you couldn't see us, you could definitely smell us.

Rusk was a stocky redhead from Kentucky. Even though he was just turning twenty-one, his voice was deep and masculine. And he had a southern accent thick enough to drown in.

"It sucks to be out here on my birthday. I ought to be gettin' drunk *and* gettin' laid tonight!" he complained bitterly.

"Well, the weekend's coming," said Avila. "You'll be up to your neck in pussy soon enough." A tall Marine of Hawaiian and Spanish descent, Avila's beautiful face and gentle manner always got him whatever girl he wanted.

The fourth man in the back of the Humvee was Ski. Lean and wiry but solidly muscular, he had a rugged, handsome face, dark hair, and steel-gray eyes.

Ski was Force-Recon, as were about one-quarter of the troops in my unit. The Recon Marines always bonded more tightly than regular Marines. They'd hang out in the squad bays in small groups and even request to be roomed together in the BEQ (Bachelor Enlisted Quarters). I'd always envied that a bit.

Two of Ski's favorite pastimes were pissing me off and showing off his dick.

He'd ask you if you wanted to see his eagle tattoo, then pull you into the back office of the equipment warehouse and drop trouser. After peeling back the foreskin and exposing his long thick cock—which seemed to somehow always be semihard—sure enough, there was the tattoo, smack dab on the top of the head.

When Ski showed me his tattoo, I said, "Did it hurt?"

"It did at first. But then afterwards it felt good."

I didn't want to betray my sexual excitement. Anyways, I'd jack off about it later.

At this point in my life, I knew I liked cock but so far I had only had sex with women and didn't identify as gay.

Sitting there in the back of the Humvee, I hit on an idea. Something that could land me in the brig if we got caught, but I was willing to take that risk. I zipped down the window to the driver and told him to make a detour to where my car was parked at our unit building. I got out, opened my trunk, and fished out a fifth of Wild Turkey. I stuffed it under some extra cammies and carried the bundle back to the Humvee. Then I announced that we were going to have a birthday party tonight and play spades. I told Rusk to bring a blanket; Avila, a lantern; and Ski, a deck of cards. At 2200, we'd all meet at a nearby gas chamber formerly used for training but now deserted.

We returned to camp, ate, and went back to our tents.

To reduce our chances of getting caught, I assigned Henderson to do first fire watch because he was notorious for falling asleep fifteen minutes into his four-hour watch.

Ski and I headed out a little bit before our rendezvous time.

It was a short hike to the gas chamber—a squat little cinder-block structure off in the rugged hills of Camp Pendleton. Avila and Rusk were already there; I could tell from the dull white light visible in the gap beneath the blanket fastened over the doorway. Ski and I entered, startling the two younger Marines.

"Okay, now we need a table," I told them.

Avila said that he had noticed some boards outside. He went to get them. Soon Ski was shuffling the cards for a good game of spades.

"No twenty-first birthday would be complete without booze," I remarked as I pulled out the bottle of Wild Turkey.

I handed the bottle to Rusk and he greedily took a long draw off it. Coughing, he passed it over to Avila. We played cards for a full hour, all the while talking about women, the Corps, and life back home. I listened to every word the others said, not saying too much myself, just drinking in their stories along with my share of the Wild Turkey.

Pretty soon Rusk was having trouble keeping his eyes open, so Avila volunteered to sneak him back into camp. Ski and I stayed in the gas chamber playing cards. As we talked, the discussion became more and more sexual.

"Buchman, what was the best sex you ever had?" "Where was the freakiest place you ever had sex?" Stuff like that. By now we had finished off the bottle. Abruptly, he laid down his cards and said, "Buchman, you ever had the urge to be *evil?*"

He stood up and began to walk over to me. We were both smashed. I got up too and backed up slightly. There was a strange and slightly sinister look in his bleary eyes as he focused on me, sizing me up.

"I mean, do you ever want to be *evil . . .*"

Ski continued advancing toward me, his eyes locked with mine and his hand rubbing over his chest.

Stumbling, he caught himself with his left hand against the wall, putting his body only a few inches from mine. I was trapped with my back against the cold cinder-block wall. His right arm brushed up against my forearm. Slowly he reached his hand to the thin fabric of my worn green T-shirt and began to massage my chest.

My mind was screaming warnings, but my cock was hard.

I was close to passing out at this point from excitement and fear, wanting him so badly but afraid of that same desire.

His hand moved to my shoulder then around to my back. I felt the heat coming off him in waves and smelled the musky scent of his body mixed with the liquor.

Like a gazelle at an African watering hole who has just noticed a lion about to strike, I panicked.

"No, Ski, I'm good. Good. I don't have an evil bone in my body," I stammered.

He wasn't the slightest bit fazed.

"Sometimes, I get the urge to be *really* evil." He drew himself even closer and pressed his legs against mine.

His closeness, my excitement, and the alcohol all combined into an overwhelming need to vomit.

I pushed past him and ran outside and threw up all the night's drinking along with the ham omelette MRE (Meal Ready to Eat) I had had for dinner.

The moment lost, we silently gathered up our stuff, went back to the bivouac site, and passed out in our cots.

We awoke the next morning, hungover but fully functional, a testament to youth. All day I privately lamented the lost opportunity for sex, but I also realized that things could have gotten complicated. Ski was, after all, married with kids. And while I was reasonably sure I knew what he'd meant by *evil,* I couldn't be certain.

After that experience, though, Ski would roughhouse with me and we'd hang out more often than before, almost like we'd developed a trust. If he had presented me with sex, I didn't take him up on it, so in his eyes I must've been straight. I felt we were able to bond on a deeper level as a result. While I may not have had sex, that experience and the times afterward left me knowing that Ski would be one of those people I'd remember until the day I die.

☆2☆

Barracks Bad Boys & Samurai Sally I: My Mormon Bad Boy

Dink Flamingo

The first barracks bad boy I want to talk about was—in terms of models, in terms of guys that I videotaped—my first love.

There used to be a GI and his wife who lived in a mobile home park which butted up against the fence to the Army post here. One of my other models took me over there one day. And when I discovered that this was where a lot of young GIs liked to hang out, I decided that I was going to like hanging out there too.

For some reason all the GIs just loved going over to this young couple's place. I think because it was so close to post, yet it was getting away from post. It wasn't a very big place; it was only a dainty little two bedroom. But they had a satellite dish hooked to the makeshift deck that all the boys had got together and built onto the trailer. So it was a very popular spot for cookouts. And any given Friday or Saturday there'd be twenty or thirty GIs at this place, out in the yard drinking beer, and in and out of the house.

Well, one particular night I was there talking with the GI's wife. The place was pretty much a madhouse. People were coming and going, and everyone was eating. I had cooked that day, on the grill. And I noticed this very, *very* cute boy, sitting in the living room by himself just watching television. He wasn't speaking to anyone, and no one was saying anything to him.

I asked the young lady, "What's his name?"

"Rob."

"Hey, Rob! How are you, man? I'm Dink." I told him, "Look, I cooked all this food. I'm gonna be heartbroken if you don't come and eat some of it." And he just got this big smile on his face.

Rob was a tall, lanky boy. Probably six feet, three inches, 165 pounds. He got up and came over, started eating. And he and I really started talking. He told me about his childhood growing up in Utah. He was from a Mormon background. And he told me how much he hated the Army, how he was in fact in trouble at that very moment, and was not supposed to be off post. He was on restriction, but he "didn't pay any attention to the fuckin' restriction." He said he came and went as he pleased and didn't give a fuck whether they put him out or not.

Honestly, at first I was a little put off by his negative attitude toward the Army. But eventually it started to become a turn-on. And the whole little bad-boy image that he had started getting to me. There was something about him that I really liked.

My conversation with him went on all evening. Finally I reached the point where I didn't care to talk anymore. I'd heard enough. I had looked at him and had lusted after him for hours, and I'd been drinking constantly. I said to myself, *Okay, now it's time. I wanna get in his pants.* So I suddenly made a big announcement to everybody that I needed cigarettes, and that I was going to have Rob take me to the store to get cigarettes.

Well, of course everybody there knew what was going on. They knew that I made porn videos, and in fact the husband was always trying to hook me up with guys because I would pay him a finder's fee for models. But the little girl, the wife, she looked at Rob as if to say, *You poor thing.*

I had not gotten any signals from Rob that would lead me to believe that I had it in the bag, so to speak. But I was going to try anyway. And I had enough alcohol in me to give me the nerve.

I will never forget getting in his car. He had a 1976 Trans Am with the seats almost entirely ripped out of it. And when he revved it up, it was the loudest thing I'd ever heard in my life. Everybody in the trailer park could hear that car! And boy, that was his pride and joy. On the back of his windshield there was a sticker that said:

I DO WHAT THE VOICES IN MY HEAD TELL ME TO DO.

So off to the store we went. He was driving crazy. I was being thrown from side to side. I thought, *Oh fuck. If I start trying to give this guy head he's going to run us into a tree!*

When we got back to the driveway of the mobile home I said, "I think I should tell you something. I really like you, Rob. I'm hoping we can be friends. But I think it's important that you know that I'm gay."

"Oh, I already knew that."

"Oh. Did Shane or his wife tell you?"

"No. I could just tell."

"Oh." I didn't ask for any further explanation.

We went back in. I was getting really tired. I decided that if anything was going to happen with him, it wasn't going to be that particular night. And Rob said that he probably ought to get back to base. I gave him my phone number.

About three days later I got a phone call. "Dink! How's it going, dude? I don't know if you remember me. I met you over at Shane's."

"Yeah, yeah, yeah—I remember you!"

"Well, dude, my car blew up today. But I'd really like to hang out, if that's cool with you."

"Aren't you supposed to be staying on post?"

"Aw, shit," he said. "I've been on restriction so long now, nobody's paying attention to what I do any more."

So I picked him up at the PX and brought him home. And we just hung out and watched movies. That's all we did. And these kinds of meetings went on for about a week. Every single day he would call me and ask if I felt like hanging out. And you know, some evenings I had other things to do. But I would still tell him, "Yes, I will be there to get you." I started putting off everything else, and everybody else, for this guy. There was something about him that I wanted to get next to. Well, I was infatuated.

Rob looked like a six-foot-three version of Macaulay Culkin. Greenish light blue eyes. Sandy blond hair. Very lanky and very tall.

Which was never my taste, before him. I'm five foot eight and I always liked them my height or shorter. And he had tattoos: a sun around one of his nipples. And above one nipple it said LOVE, and above the other one it said HATE. On one arm he had roses, and on the other arm he had thorns with blood coming off of them. And on his back he had a tattoo of a heavy metal album cover, right below his neck.

There was something about these tattoos that really turned me on. Just the fact that until he took his shirt off he looked so innocent. And I think that's what I was initially drawn to. I thought I had someone that I was going to corrupt. A beautiful, baby-faced Mormon boy. But when he took off his shirt he looked like he'd been to prison for four years. And later I would come to realize that he had done those things to his body mainly to rebel. His parents were totally against tattoos. Upsetting his parents seemed to be something he really wanted to do. That's one reason why he got in trouble in the Army, because he knew that it would really upset them.

So these visits continued. One evening as we were watching a movie he complained about his neck hurting.

"Why don't I give you a massage?"

"Okay."

I started rubbing his neck, and finally I had him just lie down on the bed. He had his shirt off, and he was wearing a pair of jogging pants cut off into shorts. I started massaging his legs, and going up his leg, getting very close to his balls. I was hoping he'd get aroused. And he did.

He rolled over and pulled down his gym shorts and his tighty whities.

"Is this what you want?"

I just kind of looked stunned for a minute. I didn't know what the right answer would be. I didn't know if it was time yet. So I said, "Oh, put that back."

He started laughing. "Oh, come on," he said, "you know you want it."

I said, "Did I say that?"

"No. But I can tell."

"Okay, you're right," I said. "I do. But I want you to know that you do not have to do that. I want you to be sure that *you* want to do it."

"I'm sure."

So he pulled it out again. I gave him a really quick blow job. He came really fast.

He immediately went to the bathroom and closed the door. I heard water running. He came back out and said, "I better get back."

I hopped up and took him back to base.

I think that he may have had immediate guilty feelings. He was unusually quiet. I think he was a little anxious about what he had done. And that he may have been slightly embarrassed about the way that he went about it.

When I pulled up to base I said, "Rob, I want you to understand something."

"What's that, man?"

"We, as men, sometimes do things out of the ordinary. But usually they're things that we want to do. You shouldn't ever beat yourself up about that. Ever. Don't ever make yourself feel bad about doing something that you thought felt good," I said. "I hope I'll hear from you soon."

"You will," he said. And he got out of the car.

And the very next day I heard from him. That surprised me. I had thought that he wouldn't call.

Well, here's the big kicker. Rob not only came over again, he decided to stay the night. Because he'd done some acid.

We closed all of the windows and made it completely dark in the house except for candles. We listened to Enya. We were massaging each other, and it was very, very intimate.

Now, this was a weekend night, and Rob had told me, "As long as I'm back by seven-thirty for extra duty I'll be fine, because nobody's checking on me."

Well, somewhere in the midst of the night we fell asleep. And I *know* that I had set the alarm clock. To this day I have always wondered if he did not turn that alarm clock off on purpose. Because when I woke up it was 8:30.

"Fuck! Rob! Get up! Get up! You got to go, man! Get up! You're late, late, late! Come on, come on, come on! You got to go!"

He looked up at me, and he said to me in this dreamy voice, "Aw, I don't wanna go back. All they're gonna do is give me forty-five more days. . . ."

Something inside of me didn't want him to go back either. And so I sat there with him, for two hours, until after ten o'clock in the morning, rationalizing with him why he shouldn't go back. And of course, by that time he was absent without leave. Rob went AWOL, and he stayed in my home.

* * *

The sex was great. He wanted to try everything. And it was the most interesting and fascinating thing. I would go off to work in the morning thinking, "I wonder what he's going to want to do this evening?" And every day when I came home there was something new he wanted to try.

I was living in a two-story house with a female roommate before he came into the picture. She allowed him to move in. She didn't ask me to increase my part of the rent or anything. We all shared the kitchen downstairs, but he and I had the entire upstairs to ourselves. And she and Rob actually got along very well.

At first while I was working he would just stay home. Clean the house, take care of the dogs. Obviously, being AWOL, he couldn't go out and get a job just anywhere. After two months I got him a job with my brother-in-law, moving mobile homes. He was willing to pay Rob under the table. He also really liked Rob a lot.

That job is very hard work. Rob was really working his ass off. He was leaving at six in the morning and sometimes not getting home until eight at night. And coming in looking like he'd been drug through hell and back.

He put all of his money into the household. Every dime he made he brought to me.

"You've been takin' care of me for a long time now. Take this."

I'd say, "No, you gotta keep some for you."

"No. You take it. I'm living okay. And you're paying for it. You take this and help pay for all this stuff."

That was nice. That made me feel good. It made me feel like he wasn't just using me.

But about three weeks after he started that job I noticed a distinct change in Rob and how he viewed our relationship. At the midpoint of the relationship Rob decided that this lifestyle was for him. That he was gay. And that he wanted us to be together. After he got this job he wasn't sure *what* was going on. He thought he might still be straight, but he wasn't sure. He knew he still liked women; he'd had sex with women before, but never any relationship.

My brother-in-law has never been all that crazy about my lifestyle. And I think that he sort of started filling Rob's head full of shit about me. Maybe it was also because after two months of being under my wing Rob had gotten back out into the real world and realized that he was once again somewhat independent. But my guess is that a lot of it had to do with my brother-in-law. He probably thought that the lifestyle was not good for Rob. And probably talked a lot of negative things about it, which I think in turn rubbed off on Rob. My brother-in-law was in his early forties. He was the father of a teenager himself. Rob wasn't much older than a teenager. My brother-in-law may also have been looking out for me in some ways, because I think he knew that the financial burden on me was strenuous. Keeping Rob up.

I was beginning to itch. I was missing the camera. I was missing all the boys. Not necessarily the sex, but I was missing the fun. And I began to feel like an old person with him. Having my whole social life shrink to just him and me. It was very hard to have outside relationships because Rob was always suspicious that I was trying to pick up the next GI. Shane was always calling me, saying, "Dink, what's up? Man, I got guys over here left and right that want to model!"

Every time the phone rang Rob would grab it. "Naw, we're not gonna do anything tonight, man. We're just gonna chill here."

One day I discovered that he had been turning the ringer off on the phone. I figured it out because people had been calling and leaving messages: "Dink, where the fuck are you? I haven't talked to you in weeks!"

Rob just said, "I didn't know it was off."

Several times I said to him, "Our friends are feeling alienated."

"Well, all those people want is this, that, and the other." He always had something to say about how they all had ulterior motives for wanting us around. At that point I listened. I thought, *Well, maybe he's right.*

The whole time we were together we had only one fight. But it was a really bad one. It happened because I went out to dinner with an old friend of mine. I had told Rob, "I'm going to go out with him by myself."

When I came back from dinner Rob immediately wanted to have sex.

Now, I had not had sex with the person that I had gone to dinner with. But Rob declared that I had come in my underwear.

"What? What are you talking about?!"

"I can tell! It's still wet!"

I started drinking. I lost my temper. He pissed me off to the point where I ran him into the bathroom. He locked the door.

"Come out of there! I'll show you a wet dick! I'll show you that you're fucking crazy!"

I was way past belligerent. I was kicking the door. And he was crying. He lay on the floor and slept in the bathroom, scared to come out because I was drunk and threatening to beat the shit out of him. I finally went to bed and got up the next morning and went to work and didn't say a word to him on the way out.

Well, that cured Rob of ever making an accusation like that again. But at the same time it also cured me of going out with anybody because I was afraid of ever going through that scene again. So when people would invite me out I would just tell them, "Man, I'm too busy." The whole situation started really getting me down. I'm a very social person. I like being with people; I like being in crowds. I started to feel claustrophobic. And I couldn't take that anymore.

Then my roommate started putting pressure on me to get rid of Rob. She saw that he was causing me a lot of stress. Not because of anything I was saying to her, but she could tell. One night she came to me and said, "Dink, what are you going to do?"

"I don't know. I don't know. I love him."

"Baby, love don't pay the bills."

Well, I told her that that was just about the brightest thing I had ever heard.

"I just don't think it's healthy for you, Dink."

"You're absolutely right."

At that moment I made up my mind: *Fuck this, I'm moving out. I'm not living with this bitch anymore. She's trying to tear us apart!*

To be honest, I had already been sort of plotting how to get her out of my life for some time. She was an undersexed paralegal, a very large woman with a bald spot. When she looked at the guys that I would bring home her eyes would pop and her mouth would literally drop open. And she was just a little too pushy about always offering her assistance in terms of taking any pictures or anything I might need while I was filming. One time I did let her take some pictures while I was filming a double jerk-off. And it was so obvious that she was getting her jollies that it really disgusted me. I didn't want the guys to feel like I was using them to help her get her rocks off. You'd think that some of the straight guys would feel more comfortable having a woman present, but not this one. They actually complained to me that she gave them the creeps.

Rob had been AWOL for four months when my brother-in-law no longer needed him because the work was slow. I told him, "Look, I think maybe it's time for you to turn yourself in."

I was surprised that he agreed so quickly.

"Don't worry about it," I said. "I'm going to be there for you."

I took him to base that same day and dropped him off outside the provost marshall's office. And just kept driving, because he'd said, "There's no need for you to stop here. I don't want you to get tangled up in this."

An hour and a half later he called me up. "Guess what? They're flying me to Fort Knox tonight."

"What? That quick?"

"Yeah, they're just gonna drop me off at the airport," he said. "Can you come and let's have something to eat while I'm waiting on my plane?"

So I went to the airport. And we had something to eat there in the diner. I told him, "Don't you worry." I said, "I'll drive to Kentucky. You just call me and let me know when you're getting out, and I will be there waiting for you."

Sure enough, just four days later he called me up and said, "I'll be released on Friday."

So of course, I was there. As a matter of fact, I pulled up about five minutes before they released him. He came out and there I was sitting in the parking lot in my car.

On my way there I'd gone through the mountains of North Carolina. It was about a fourteen-hour drive. And I thought how wonderful it would be for us to come back through the mountains, for him to see all of this.

We had a great trip back. He, of course, was elated to be out. And I was glad that it was all over and that he didn't have to duck his head anymore. And we took this long journey through the mountains of North Carolina. Went to the swinging bridge over Grandfather Mountain, and Blowing Rock, and all of these special places. Just had a really, really lovely trip.

When we came back I was in the middle of moving into my own place. I knew that Rob didn't have any higher education. I knew that, at best, he was going to get minimum-wage jobs, having just gotten put out of the Army with an Other Than Honorable discharge.

A lot of things really started to hit me and sink in.

"Rob," I said, "now it's time to call your parents. Because I'm sure they are worried sick about you. You need to let your family know where you're at." I had tried and tried to get him to call them, but he had not spoken to his parents this entire time.

"Okay, I will," he said. "But can I wait and do it tomorrow?"

"Okay. But you need to do it."

And so the next day he called them. He talked to his mother, his brother, his sister, and his father. I went outside. I didn't listen to the conversation. When I came back in he seemed to be feeling good. I was hoping that the conversation with his family would go well. The entire time outside I was thinking: *I hope he wants to go home.* And I was confused, because I didn't know why I felt that way. But what I told myself at the time was that I needed for him to go home and let me make this move and get us settled, and then bring him back.

I didn't say anything. I waited to see if he would come up with the idea on his own.

He never made the suggestion. Things just went on as usual. We watched movies that night together, lying on the couch, and went to bed, and made love, and nothing was said.

The next day at work I thought about it all day. I made up my mind that I was going to tell him. I rehearsed my story. And so after I got home and we were eating I said, "Rob, how would you like to go home and visit the family for a couple of weeks?"

He got this really terrible look on his face.

"Oh, no. No," he said. "I don't want to."

"Are you sure? It would give me time to get us moved. You could go and visit them," I said. "And then when you come back we'll have our own place."

"Are you sure you're gonna want me to come back?"

"I'm positive I'm gonna want you to come back."

"Well, I'm not going unless you promise me that I can come back."

"I promise you can come back."

"Well, how long?" He said, "I don't know if I can stand it for two weeks."

"Let's say two weeks at the max."

Reluctantly, he agreed. The next day I got Rob a plane ticket. I wound up borrowing the money from my old friend Beau, who was always very supportive of my relationship with Rob.

I'll never forget standing at the airport that night. Before we left the house, he went outside and took a piece of newspaper with him.

He came back in, and he had something wrapped up in the newspaper.

"What is that?"

"Oh, nothin'. I just want to take something home from North Carolina."

We got to the airport, we were sitting down at the gate talking. And he opened up the newspaper and said, "Here." And what he gave me was a limb and the leaves and the flower from a magnolia tree.

"That's the only flower I could find."

I told him that it was beautiful.

"Do you know why I've always loved you?" he asked.

I said, "No, why?"

"Because you paid me attention."

"What do you mean?"

"Do you remember the very first night you met me at that trailer? When all those people were going in and out and nobody was talking to me? You were the first person to talk to me that night. From that night on until now you have done nothing but give me your undivided attention. That's why I love you." And he said, "I'm coming back here!"

"I know you are."

When he got on that plane, somehow in my heart I knew I'd never see him again.

* * *

Well, of course it's true that I didn't give him a round-trip ticket.

As much as I did want him back, I knew that it was a bad idea. But I felt good about where I was leaving him. I had gotten him home. I felt like I had done my duty to him.

I've always felt bad about that alarm clock not going off that morning. As I said, many times after that I wondered if he had woken up when I was still asleep and turned it off on purpose. But I also always felt a certain amount of guilt because I thought maybe I didn't turn it on, and maybe it was because of me that he was late, and therefore because of me he went AWOL. But at the end of it all I felt like I had done my part. I felt like I had done everything that was right. I had helped that kid. I had fed that kid. I had done everything I could to make sure that from the time he went AWOL to the time he got on the plane that night he was well taken care of and he knew somebody loved him.

And I felt like I'd sacrificed an important part of my life, which was being with all of my GIs, and being sort of that one-man USO they all would come to. Which had by this point become defunct because I was off in another world with Rob. After that was over, I'll never forget all those guys telling me, "We thought we would never get you back."

Beau, on the other hand, still to this day talks about that relationship. About how in love Rob was with me, and how obvious it was that I was in love with Rob. He says it was one of the most beautiful things that he has ever sat back and watched.

"Dink, if anybody has ever loved you, it was Rob."

I believe him. I trust his observation. I also think that his vicarious pleasure in watching our relationship was the only reason he loaned me the money to send Rob to visit his family.

But the next story I'm going to tell you has to do with Beau, and a barracks bad boy that I ended up having to take off of Beau's hands and *fix*.

☆3☆

Smoking Guns

Daniel Luckenbill

In 1970 and just out of the Army, I got a job that didn't pay very much, so I joined the Reserves. Once again I stood at attention in my dress uniform with medals before a commanding officer. "You are a well-decorated young lieutenant," he said, returning my salute and welcoming me.

That summer our unit went to Fort Leavenworth, Kansas, home to the military prison for the Army's worst offenders. On a tour of the prison I stood in awed silence as a sergeant showed us the shower room, immense and flooded with light. I felt the sergeant's eyes lock with mine as he recited the details of how prisoners were stripped down here. I imagined bodies moving defiantly under water spraying from the gleaming steel spigots. At this time of day the gray concrete room and tiers of cells were empty. But somewhere in this prison there was one soldier that I knew. The most handsome GI that I'd met in my three years on active duty, Wyatt Mackey.

☆ ☆ ☆

In the winter of 1969 I sat alone in the Trade Winds bar in Lawton, Oklahoma, against the wall in a booth where I nursed a beer and could see the GIs playing pool at the far end of the room. It was my last night in the Army and my last night in town. The low-hanging lamp over the pool table illuminated only the midsections of their bodies. Trim stomachs, tight thighs, and the sex between. One tall GI stood back from the table, blurred in a smoky haze. When his turn came he held his pool stick upright before him as he put chalk on its tip. He bent into the light. The thrust of his shoulder blades pulled up his shirt, the movement of his body stretched the fabric of his pants tightly over his ass. The thick end of the cue jerked backward. I heard the sound of one ball striking another, and one thumping into a pocket. He was too far away for our eyes to meet, but I felt that he could sense my presence, my glances turned to his game.

This was how I'd passed my off-duty hours in the months since returning from Vietnam, stationed back at Fort Sill my last three months in the Army. Instead of hanging out with fellow officers, I spent my evenings mingling with enlisted men at the country bars and go-go joints in the downtown combat zone, looking for trade. There were Marines at Sill for artillery training, there were Army privates fresh off the farm out blowing their first small paychecks. I'd just bought a new red sports car and could give these boys a ride to the roadhouse and buy them beer. I listened to their stories. They weren't used to that. When the bars closed, I could offer them a ride back to post and even a place to crash. I had strategically chosen not to stay at the popular new high-rise Bachelor Officer Quarters but in a quieter part of the base where I wouldn't be under close scrutiny.

The GI that I'd been watching headed toward the men's room. I followed. He had a great style. He stood well back from the urinal and, with one arm extended, fell forward and braced his left hand against the wall. Using only his right hand he unzipped his fly and flopped out his cock.

Uncut. The excess skin wrinkled and pinched together at the end.

He looked straight ahead, as if he knew I would glance his way and he would permit it. He gave his cock a few extra flips, pulled back the skin until the head was fully exposed, then let it inch back.

"Yank my doodle, it's a dandy," he said to the wall in front of him.

He zipped up with the same style. With just one flip his cock vanished back into the folds of his trousers.

I let him wash his hands first and get back to his pool game. But when I returned he had taken the other seat in my booth. His beer bottle was next to mine on the table.

"Mind if I rest here awhile?"

"No, please, go right ahead."

He moved his bottle a little closer to mine.

This was happening too fast.

He looked toward the soft green light reflected from the now vacant pool table.

"Slow night," he said, shifting my way. The full features of his face contradicted the tautness of his body. His almost-shaved head made his bright eyes appear larger than they really were. He took a sip from his beer and not so subtly turned the bottle so the light would shine through it.

"Can I buy you a beer?"

With a flashing grin that made his full lips open wide, he said, "I thought you'd never ask." He scooted himself all the way into the booth and stretched out his long legs over the seat, his cowboy boots hanging over into the room.

"Glenda!" He called the waitress to our booth. Turning his eyes under his dark lashes at her, he put his arm around her legs, then deftly moved his hand up under her miniskirt and squeezed her rear end.

"Wyatt Mackey!" She swatted his hand away. "You stop that! Hear?!"

"Aw, you know you like it. You don't really want me to stop, do you?"

"That's what I said, that's what I meant," she snapped and walked away, pouting and swinging her ass.

Now I knew his name. "Why's she wearin' that flimsy li'l thing then, if a man's not supposed to grab her?" Her rejection put Wyatt in a foul mood. His face was set with anger.

Then, looking at me: "You got a car?"

"Yes."

"Well, then, let's go."

"What?"

"Let's go for a ride or something. I've had enough of these broads for one night."

Why not leave with him? Wasn't that what I wanted? I decided not to question it.

As we moved out into the fresh cold air, Wyatt muttered, "Damn women. Drive you to drink."

"Yes. I know what you mean."

I led him to my car and unlocked the passenger door.

"Damn! Nice car! What's your name, sir?"

He'd noticed the decal marking me as an officer.

"Well, shit, Dan," he said. "I wish I'd known before now you'd buy a guy a beer now and then." He gave me a soft charming smile. "Say, how about lettin' me drive? Sure would love to get the feel of it."

"I don't usually let anyone—" I faltered. "Maybe later. Where are we going? Where am I going to buy you that beer?"

"You know what?" Wyatt yawned. "I'm kinda tired. Only I don't really have any place to stay."

It couldn't have been a better opening for me. I told him I had a sofa. Wyatt stretched back in the comfortable passenger seat and relaxed. But when he realized that we were headed for Fort Sill's main gate, he squirmed nervously in his seat.

"Dan, I didn't tell you. I can't go on base!"

"You've got your ID, haven't you?"

"Yeah, but I can't show it."

"Why is that?"

"AWOL."

Hearing that he was absent without leave made me nervous. He sensed it.

"Dan, you don't have to worry about me. I'm no big criminal or nothin'. Just AWOL."

Wyatt had me pull off to the side of the road. He lay down in the small space behind the two seats and directed me to cover him with my jacket. I slowed for the MP at the gate who saluted me and gave a quick look inside the car before waving me through.

"Best way to go AWOL," Wyatt declared, emerging from beneath the coat, "is to stay right here in Lawton. Just don't go home. They'll be right there. Especially in Arkansas. Sheriff on you, waitin' to nab you!"

I was silent.

"Sure can't wait to crawl into bed." Wyatt's lips curved in a sly grin.

I couldn't be sure what game he was playing. He seemed to have understood my interest in him. But maybe once in my room he really would just plop down on the sofa and go to sleep.

"Not bad," he said of my quarters. "Glad I met you! I'll sleep good here."

"Well, I'm leaving tomorrow. . . ."

It was as if he didn't hear me. Wyatt sat down on the bed and took off all his clothes. "Ain't you comin' to bed?"

"I don't know." I looked away and stood stiffly by the window. I stole a glance at his stark white ass as he threw back the thin bedspread and jumped into bed. After a moment I took off my clothes and sat on the edge of the bed.

I studied the form of his body beneath the sheet: chest, arms, hipbones, the curve of his thigh. He twisted and I could see his cock, hard, pushing up the sheet. I moved my body closer to his warmth, moved my hand just to brush his thigh.

He looked into my eyes, smugly recognizing my desire. I wanted to hold off but couldn't stop my hand. I grasped his hard-on. The triumph on his face was too much to bear. I moved my hand away.

"Not in the mood yet, huh?"

"No." I resented him saying yet.

He pulled his arm out from under the sheet and grabbed me tightly by the back of the neck, lifting, pushing my face down to his cock.

This was not the kind of sex I preferred, but the first few moments were good. Fitting my mouth around the head, drawing the foreskin back over it with my lips. He arched his body, thrusting the full length of his cock down my throat. His hand still held the back of my neck, gripping me even tighter. I moved my hand over the tight muscles of his thighs and cupped his balls.

I breathed hard, then couldn't breathe. My eyes watered as I choked. He jackknifed upward, relentless fast thrusts into the back of my throat until he came. His fingers pulled at the short hairs on the back of my neck, then relaxed. The fingers felt warm. Now I didn't want this to be over with. I could breathe again. The softening cock filled my mouth satisfyingly. I held my mouth tightly around him until he sat up.

"You gonna give me some money?"

I couldn't sense how demanding his question was. I decided to play it cool. "We hadn't discussed that."

"Well, I just figured. You knowin' I was broke and all."

Now I wanted to use my power over him. Just kick him out the door. It would be a long walk to the main gate for an AWOL soldier.

For a moment he looked worried. But it occurred to me that if he did get caught at the gate, he could very easily cause some trouble for me.

"I gotta eat." He reached for his cigarettes. "Wouldn't you know it?" Wyatt smiled as he showed me the now empty pack of Kools.

"I can give you ten," I told him.

"Anything you say. Since I didn't go about this quite business-like."

"I still have to finish packing," I thought out loud.

"Where are you gonna go, after tomorrow?" Wyatt asked. He was already lamenting the loss of his newfound source of income.

"I haven't completely made up my mind yet. Maybe before I head home I'll take a trip somewhere."

"Where to?" he asked, trying hard not to sound too interested.

I told him I had lived in Los Angeles, but that I might go back to see my family in Illinois, even though my mother was now living in California.

"What's your mama do, Danny?"

"Nothing, now."

"My mama works at the chicken plant. Never knew anyone to work so hard."

A chicken plant . . . I had a vague picture of an assembly line where pieces of poultry were magically assembled in plastic wrappings.

Wyatt was fondling his cock, pulling the foreskin back and forth over the head.

"Looks like George is ready again," he announced.

"George?"

"That's George." He gave his cock a playful slap. "I was fourteen the first time—the first time George got any."

"Who with?"

"This older man. Used to see me after school. He had a great car, a Buick. He liked me and this friend of mine. Took us out some country road somewhere. Said he'd give us five dollars each time. I made fifteen the first night!"

"You're kidding."

"Nope. Gospel truth. 'Course I had played around before. Girl from Missouri. George likes pussy, but he's got used to things. Ain't particular."

I moved my hand to cup his shoulder. He brushed it away.

"Look at this here," he said. He gripped his bicep underneath the blue lines spelling out MOTHER. He kneaded the muscle, as if its tension held some deeply private ache. I eased his hand away and massaged him. "It's kind of a silly tattoo," he continued. "I guess I was thinking about Arkansas when I had it done. About Mama."

"More than about your father?"

"No dad. I'm a bastard."

I felt the need to say something simple and heartfelt. "Well, it doesn't look silly to me. I wish I had a tattoo."

"My brother James, he got a pair of dice." Wyatt rolled over onto his stomach and let his body relax into the soft mattress. One arm reached out toward me, as if he would sink if he didn't touch me.

"Danny, is Nebraska on the way to Illinois?"

"What? No. It isn't."

"I was just thinking, maybe I could go up there and see that friend of mine, John. Maybe John could look after me, like he used to."

Wyatt told me the story. "Used to" was four years ago. John had "looked after him" for the same favors I was receiving.

"Until we got arrested."

He was vague about the details, but the upshot was that Wyatt had lied to the court and John was imprisoned for having homosexual relations with a minor.

"It was either him or me," Wyatt concluded.

"What makes you think he'll want you back?"

"Hell, it was only six months. I still get letters from him. Money, sometimes."

He rolled over and reached down to his pants on the floor. He produced a color Polaroid Land camera picture of himself, frayed and bent from being in his wallet for so long. It was a nude photo.

"Looked pretty good then."

In the picture he was sitting on an ornate, carved gilt chair covered in brown and white cowhide. His legs were spread, and his cock hung just over the edge of the seat. I was struck by the contrast between his beautiful dark foreskin and the bright glints of gold from the camera flash.

"John took that picture. Nice place he's got, huh?"

The room was white and simple, shuttered windows in the background. Small plants in pots. I thought the room looked like it ought to be in San Francisco, not Nebraska. I would like an apartment like that. But it was Wyatt who brought the room to life. No wonder the man kept sending him money.

Turning off the nightstand light, I decided I would drive Wyatt to Nebraska.

☆ ☆ ☆

No sooner than the first mile down the highway out of Lawton Wyatt informed me that he didn't want to go to Nebraska after all. He wanted to go to Arkansas.

I deliberated. "Would I just let you off in your hometown?" I asked.

"Nah. You could stay the night. We could get a motel."

I thought of the warmth of his tight body. Another night with Wyatt.

When we arrived at his mother's modest house she had just got off work. Wyatt had inherited her fine features, but she looked tired from her day's work. She made us dinner and insisted we spend the night there. She put quilts on a bed in a room off the kitchen. Closing the door on us, she said, "You boys sleep good now."

When I awoke the room was very cold. I tried to fall back asleep, but there was a bright sun streaming through the curtainless windows. I could see icicles on the house next door, patches of snow in the leafless trees.

Then Wyatt woke up. He looked at me with sleepy eyes and, with a frown, pulled the quilt closer against the cold. But then as he surveyed the room his expression changed. He was at home; he was reassured. He moved his face close to mine. He nestled his head against my shoulder and smiled. It wasn't emotion that he wanted from me. I felt his hard prick brush mine.

We passed the day driving around his hometown, with Wyatt now behind the wheel. Seeing the places where he'd grown up brought back fond memories, and he smiled as he pointed out where he'd gone to school, where his mother still went every Sunday to church. And he slowed to show me the liquor store that he and his brother James had robbed.

"I was sixteen when we robbed that store. It's on account of that I'm in the Army."

"Oh, you're in the Army?" I joked. "Haven't seen you at reveille lately."

He gave a short broken laugh. I'd made a mistake. There was pain on his face, and he was silent. I didn't know what to say.

"Well, aren't you going to ask me about the robbery?"

"Only if you want to talk about it."

"That was something all right." He pushed against the accelerator as he relived the memory. "James 'n me had stole a car. Hot-wired it. Just an ol' Chevy, but it run good. Fast, anyhow. Figured we had a good chance of gettin' away. But you already know that Chevy wasn't fast enough. Judge said it was reform school or the Army. Dumb me, I picked the Army."

His mother wasn't home when we got back. Wyatt announced that he was going to take a shower. He took off his shirt. I touched the soft cotton of his undershirt, his body so warm beneath it. He allowed me to hug him, hold him. When I put my hand on his crotch his cock was hard. He didn't discourage me from touching it, squeezing it. He reached for his cigarettes, lit one, and blew out the match. I inhaled smoke and sulfur as I pressed my lips against his. He tolerated this kiss.

"In the mood, huh?"

"How'd you tell."

"Can't get enough of old George, can you?"

"You know I can't."

"It's good to hear it."

As Wyatt undid his belt I reached under his thighs and felt the hard muscles. He sat down on the bed and lifted his legs for me to pull off his jeans and cotton briefs. He left his legs raised as I massaged his naked thighs. I gripped them from below and moved my mouth to his asshole. When I looked up, he was jerking off. I pulled Wyatt to me, tugged and kneaded his buttocks, sticking in my tongue as deep as it would go, enlarging the hole more and more until my tongue was no longer enough. I pushed my nose at the opening slick with saliva. My tongue snaked in circles, then my nose pushed again until it was buried in the tight clasping folds. Wyatt arched his back and exhaled strongly. He jerked himself faster, and so did I. We shot together.

He tousled my hair, and said, "You really know how to do that, buddy."

In my head it was as if he'd said, "I love you."

"Now go turn on the shower for me," he ordered. "Hurry up! Mama'll be comin' home."

At dinner Wyatt informed his mother and me that he was going with me to Illinois and that we would be leaving at eight.

Standing in the snow beside the car, she tried to persuade him to stay at least until the next day. "Those roads're gonna be covered with ice. You're not gonna see anything when it's so dark."

"Exactly. And nobody's gonna see who's in this car."

"Oh, you think everyone in town doesn't know you're back?" his mother asked.

"You hear some people talkin' about me?" This attention made him brighten.

"Why, everybody's seen this snazzy red car!" She hunched her worried face lower through the window and asked, "How come you're not drivin', Dan?"

"He don't know the roads around here like I do, Mama. Case we have to make a quick getaway."

"Getaway from what?" she asked in alarm, echoing the question in my mind.

"You just said people know I'm here."

With exaggerated caution to reassure his mother, Wyatt slowly backed the car out of the driveway.

"Take care, y'hear?" she called out to us. "Maybe you can stop here again on your way back from Illinois!" There was little hope in her voice.

The porch light went out as he backed into the street. For a moment the living-room light still shone out onto the porch and the snow, then the house was dark.

Wyatt sped through the empty streets, everything closed up for the night. Just outside the city limits he took a dangerous curve as fast as he could. He kept looking in the rearview mirror. He seemed almost disappointed that there wasn't a single police car to be seen anywhere.

I was relieved to be out of the town. I had started worrying that at any moment the sheriff might arrive and arrest Wyatt. And me too, for harboring an AWOL soldier during wartime.

He slowed as we came to a roadside Tastee-Freez stand. The parking lot was empty. In the brightly lit interior there was only one figure.

"Good. I don't know this guy. He won't recognize me."

"Isn't it a little too cold for ice cream?"

"Jesus, are you dumb," he said. "That's not what I want. C'mon."

"It's freezing. I'll just wait here."

"Come *on!* I want you with me."

We went up to the takeout window. I was rubbing my hands together to keep warm. Wyatt leaned forward against the window, trying to block the young man's admiring glances at my car.

"Two cones," Wyatt said.

"No, just one," I said, shivering.

He gave me a nudge. Out of view of the Tastee-Freez boy's eyes, under the takeout window shelf, Wyatt let me see the pistol in his hand. He grinned at me.

My heart started pounding.

"Wyatt . . . don't . . . I can't . . . I'm not—"

The young man finished teasing the soft white cream into a cone with a fancy little twirl at the top.

"Pay the man," Wyatt told me. My shaking hand dug into my pocket for change. Wyatt put the gun back into his baggy pants.

As we continued down the highway I was unable to speak for some minutes. Licking his tongue around the ice cream cone, Wyatt was plainly relishing the shock he'd given me.

"That woulda been easy," he said, wiping off his mouth.

"And it would have been easy for us to get caught, too," I said. "You're crazy."

"Oh, is that what you think? You think I'm crazy?"

I had used the wrong word. He rolled down the window and threw out the stub of the cone. He pulled the gun from his pocket, unlocked the safety, and fired the pistol out into night three times. He put it between our seats. I gripped it to check the safety. The barrel was smoking hot and burned my hand.

His hand was still sticky from the ice cream, and he wiped it on the thigh of my pants and left it there. In spite of my anger, I got an erection. He didn't look at me, his eyes were on the road. But his hand squeezed gently. He unzipped my pants, pulled out my hard-on, and gripped it with force. After just a few quick strokes I started to come. He let go of me and returned his hand to the wheel. I had to finish by myself. He didn't want to get it on his hands.

"Now don't say I never done nothing for you."

A flash in the rearview mirror struck his eyes.

"Dammit. You got me all distracted." He eased his foot from the gas pedal. The headlights behind us drew closer. Then the driver turned off down a side road.

Wyatt grunted and resumed speeding. Instead of relief, he seemed to be feeling disappointment.

"Are you looking for a chase? You know, I almost think you want to get picked up by that sheriff."

"Huh?"

"Wyatt, why don't you just turn yourself in?"

"What kind of stupid question is that? Why would *anybody* want to be in Leavenworth?"

"I think you just want to get it over with."

He was silent for a moment. "Well, I didn't get picked up. Lucked out again."

Another mile or so down the road he asked, "You said your mama was in California, not in Illinois, didn't you? And you like bein' in California better than Illinois?"

I told him that I had never felt like a human being until I'd left Illinois.

"That's what I been thinkin'. That maybe you'd just wanna go on back to California instead of makin' this long drive to Illinois first."

I had to laugh at this latest twist to Wyatt's plan.

"I'm sure you wanna see your mama. And if I was to go with you I could do the drivin'. We'd be out there in no time."

More time with Wyatt. How could I say no?

"So whaddya say?"

"Sure."

"Good. That way tomorrow on the way back through Lawton I can stop by and see this girl Cindy I know. Lives in Cache, outside Lawton. Can't really leave for California without sayin' good-bye to Cindy."

Wyatt turned the car around and drove straight through to Oklahoma. We got the last room at a very cheap motel Wyatt knew outside of town.

"All I care about is that it's got a bed," he said.

He lay down on top of the worn green chenille bedspread. He stripped down to his T-shirt. I moved close beside him. I touched his forehead. He pushed my hand away.

"You must be tired, driving all this way."

"No shit."

"Damn it, Wyatt. I'm trying to be nice to you."

He looked surprised to hear me curse.

"You are. I'm sorry." I nuzzled his cheek with mine.

"Ouch!" he said. "Your beard scratches. You need to go shave."

When I returned from the bathroom I half expected to find him asleep, but he was sitting up in bed smoking a Kool.

"Danny, what's California really like? I mean, you think I could find a . . . find some kind of work out there right away?"

"Why not? But even if you don't, I'm sure I can get a job and make enough . . . probably enough for the two of us to manage."

He looked me directly in the eye. "I want to do more than just get by."

His stare was oddly intense. Then he turned away from me, rolled over on his side, and stared at the wall. I didn't say anything to disturb his thoughts. I didn't want to risk again uttering some word that would touch some nerve.

"Shit!" Wyatt exclaimed.

"What's the matter?"

"Everything's the matter." He let out a strong breath to disguise his deep feelings. "Danny . . ." Slowly he turned back to face me. "Danny, what am I gonna do when you get tired of me?"

After the pause was already too awkward, I told him, "I won't get tired of you." I put my arm around him.

He didn't ask for any further reassurance.

I smelled the moist cloth covering his armpits. His sweat mixed with the fresh soapy smell of the T-shirt his mother had washed for him. The scent was intoxicating. I helped him off with his T-shirt, and the odor of his body was stronger. In a second he had his boots off, his jeans and briefs. His cock was hard, arching. He opened his mouth to speak, but I was already taking off my clothes.

"George is ready."

He knelt on the bed for me to move under him. I reached up to his cock.

"Roll over," he told me.

My flesh resisted the first jab. *No, it's too large,* I thought. Then: *No, give it to me, fuck me, give me all of it.* I forced my insides to fit his cock. With each withdrawing motion I clenched him more tightly.

His continued plunges, the sweat from his chest on my back—my skin began to quiver. *Hold down my shoulders, stop my arms from shaking,* I wanted to say. My convulsing made him thrust down harder, pinning me down. I moved as he wanted me to move and I couldn't move without him. No thought but the motion inside me.

I shot onto the bed beneath me.

He began to turn his body from mine, but I turned with him, his cock still in my ass. When he pulled out, my muscles strained to close around the nothing that was there.

Wyatt slept, but I couldn't. I switched off the light but hated the darkness. I got out of bed and picked up the keys where Wyatt had thrown them down. I felt an impulse to leave. I could simply walk out the door, turn the key in the ignition. Leave a note. Wyatt could go see that damn girl Cindy. He was where he belonged. He needed to turn himself in.

I was in love with him; I was sure of that. Wyatt didn't trust my love. If he didn't, why should I? I had never been with anyone long enough for the strength of my feelings to be tested. In the Army guys were always being transferred out. In Vietnam they died. GIs in Lawton stopped coming around to the bars where I'd met them or would come back only with buddies. Or ship out to another post. One or two went to the stockade.

I didn't want to wake Wyatt. I quietly returned my car keys to the table and crawled back into bed. The bedclothes over Wyatt moved as he breathed. I didn't want such sights, such intimacy ever to end.

We slept until about checkout time. I woke to see Wyatt walking naked into the bathroom. When he finished, it was my turn to shower and I watched him in the mirror as he sat down on the edge of the bed to put on his socks. His legs spread, his cock long. It was a pose like the picture he'd shown me. I was thrilled with this image. I would be seeing this show every day with him in California.

I stepped naked out of the bathroom. Wyatt stood by the door. He'd already jumped into his clothes and had put on my jacket. His arms hung stiffly at his side, jerked forward uncertainly as I stood before him. I could see he wanted to make some movement toward me but was unable. His lips parted slightly in the middle. We leaned toward each other, as if we might kiss. Then with great effort he raised his arms toward my shoulders. When I did the same he let his arms drop, and this motion too I imitated. There was no kiss.

"Where's the keys?" I felt he could read my thoughts of leaving him last night.

"Where you left them."

He drove me into town and we arranged to meet later after he'd seen Cindy.

Wyatt didn't want to go back to the Trade Winds bar. "How about the Oriental?" he asked. "Nine o'clock."

I wandered aimlessly around the town I thought I'd said good-bye to. Since I had allowed Wyatt to take my jacket I had to put on my Army field jacket. I felt awkward wearing it with jeans. It was against regulations, and even though I was now out of the Army, the people in this military town didn't know that.

The jacket's decorations were reduced to mere color: the bright yellow Cav patch, the blue CIB, the silver lieutenant bars all lost their significance. Even my name embroidered on the jacket now seemed meaningless to me. I felt stripped of my military identity—my masculine identity. Any identity.

I arrived at the Oriental well before nine and ordered a drink as I waited for Wyatt. I waited until ten . . . eleven . . . until it was after midnight and I realized that any thoughts of his being late were just wishful thinking. I had set myself up perfectly.

☆ ☆ ☆

I never called the police, afraid that I might be accused of aiding a deserter. I didn't have enough traveler's checks to pay for a plane ticket, so I returned to Los Angeles by bus.

Six weeks later I received a phone call from the vice president of the bank in Lawton that had financed the car. I had made two more payments, since I didn't want to answer the questions they'd ask if I told them the car had been stolen by an AWOL hustler.

The vice president told me the car had been returned because it had been part of an armed robbery somewhere in Arkansas. The robber had been caught. I didn't ask about him, since I still wasn't sure about letting them know I knew Wyatt.

"It's lucky for you the guy tried to rob that bank," he said. "Otherwise you might never have got your car back."

I took a plane to Oklahoma. The car was in storage at a greasy auto shop on the highway outside Lawton. It had been stripped of its spare tire. The headlights were damaged and would never again work quite right. Missing were my camera and some pictures of GIs I'd known before Wyatt. Gone, too, was a blue sweater that my mother had knit me. In the backseat was a pair of shit-stained men's briefs.

The mechanic who showed me the damage couldn't get over the fact that the car antenna had been shot off. "That sure is crazy, the sheriff shootin' off that antenna!"

"According to the sheriff 's report, he was aiming for the gas tank, hoping to blow up the car."

"And blow up the driver!"

"And blow up the driver," I echoed.

"Good thing he missed!"

He looked at me, unable to understand my expression. His eyes were wide with excitement over a thrilling chase scene. I was fighting back tears.

"You best buy a new spare tire for your trip back to California."

He sold me a tire. My savings account was now almost empty. When I got back to Los Angeles I would need to find a job quickly.

Wyatt wouldn't have to worry about finding a job for years.

☆4☆

Barracks Bad Boys & Samurai Sally II: America's Most Wanted

Dink Flamingo

The next story I'm going to tell you is about a young man who thought he was a Billy Badass. Everything about him—his walk, his talk—was badass. He was a big boy, about six foot six. And everybody in town was afraid of him. When he was off duty he bounced at the clubs.

Seth was the barracks bad boy who thought he could get over on every gay guy in town until he met Dink Flamingo.

When I first became acquainted with my good friend Beau, and for quite a few years after, he lived about twenty miles out in the country, with his wife. After his marriage ended Beau moved into the city here. He got a condo and spent a ridiculous amount of money having these wild crazy people decorate it. And he had a bevy of GIs there. He found a roommate who was one of these busybody queens that really knows how to get out and mingle, and he was quite crafty at getting boys over to Beau. It was this roommate who brought Seth to him.

Seth was a very tall, dark-haired boy, with very beautiful light brown eyes, from Emporia, Virginia. He was an infantryman and was also Airborne qualified. Seth was a GI, but he looked more like your quintessential Marine. He had a high-and-tight haircut and he kept the sides completely shaved. He looked like a twenty-two-year-old Marine version of "Bull" from *Night Court*.

Well, Beau's roommate was absolutely in love with this kid. But apparently the kid was not giving him any play. He wouldn't let him have anything. Nor would he let Beau do anything with him either.

One night Beau called me over and said, "I've got somebody I think you'll be interested in working with." So I went over and met the kid.

Seth wasn't really my type. Although I could tell he thought he was *everybody's* type.

I personally don't like them that tall. But I think I sensed something about his personality that turned me off. I immediately recognized his arrogance. It's not that he wasn't good-looking. I thought that he was great material for a model and that a lot of people would probably be as infatuated with him as Beau's roommate was.

Beau had a Polaroid camera. He said, "Here, take a few pictures on this." So I took a few shots of the guy. Got him naked, got him hard.

In the middle of this little photo session, when Beau was out of earshot, the guy said to me, "Where are you going when you leave here?"

"I'm going home."

"Do you mind if I come over there with you and we can do a little more work or whatever?"

So Seth came over to the house. And sort of moved in. I let him start staying there even though he was not my type. Of course, at that time I had so many guys staying with me it was almost like I was running a GI hostel.

And he did in fact model for me. Not very much, but this is the great part of it: Seth had sworn to Beau, and to the roommate, that he would *never* suck a dick. He would never do that. He would never put a penis in his mouth.

One night I had a female friend of mine over, and one of my other models. And the female friend started getting wild. All of a sudden I was sitting there filming Seth sucking this other model off. Until the guy came, and came all in Seth's eye.

I ended up giving that footage to Beau. And Beau just cherishes that tape, because of everything that happened.

Seth and I had sex only once. And that was also in a threesome situation, with this same other model, who was sort of a flirtatious type and would instigate things. Seth wasn't great. It was very forgettable sex.

Of course I'm probably saying things based upon how I feel about him now.

☆ ☆ ☆

During the three or four weeks that Seth was staying at my place, somebody kept breaking into Beau's house. During the day, while he was at work. And stealing stuff. Odds and ends. Nothing extremely valuable, but things that were precious to Beau. Like a wineglass that Edgar Allan Poe had drank out of. Things like that. But whoever the thief was, he was breaking in *with a key.*

By this time Beau had gotten rid of the roommate, because of all the riffraff he was bringing over. The roommate was not really a suspect for these break-ins, for a number of reasons, including the fact that he was a highly paid executive with an apparel company.

One night I called up Beau and announced that I had decided I was going to start collecting wine.

"I've got six bottles so far," I told him. "I'm gonna come over, and we're gonna pick one and have it."

And I will tell you how long my wine-collecting stage lasted. Every bit of about the end of that night! We drank all six bottles. And by the time I left there Beau had me convinced it was Seth who was ripping him off.

Beau believed that his roommate had given Seth a key. But there was also the fact that Seth was a locksmith.

"I don't have total proof yet," Beau said. "So you cannot say anything. Promise me you won't say anything! Not until I can get some kind of proof."

"I'm not gonna say anything." Well, six bottles of wine later . . .

I get back home and who should I find waiting in my driveway but Seth. He's sitting there asleep in his beat-up red '87 Thunderbird. I had not given him the key to my house. I was always a little wary about giving people keys to my home.

I go over and wake him up. He gets out of his car. I start yelling at him, "You've been rippin' Beau off!"

"What are you talkin' about?"

"I know you've been rippin' Beau off. You're a fuckin' thief!"

He says, "What's all that got to do with you?"

"It has a lot to do with me! Beau's a good friend of mine! You're gonna get your shit and get the fuck out of my house!"

So he comes in and he's huffing around. He thinks that because he's so fucking big and has been a bouncer at a couple of bars that everybody is scared of him. Well, with that much wine in me, I'm not scared of anybody. You can put anybody in my face.

He starts getting mouthy. He hesitates getting his stuff.

"I *told* you to get on back there and get your mess and get the hell out of here!"

But he just keeps standing around, running his mouth, until finally I pick up a kitchen chair and whack him right over the head with it. It's a solid pine wood chair. The back of it breaks off, and he falls to the floor.

I commence to saying, "I'm gonna kick your ass! Get the fuck on up! Come on! Get your shit and get out of my house!"

He gets up and goes to the bedroom to get his stuff.

Now, it so happens that I had a samurai sword that one of the soldiers had given me. And I had achieved the nickname of "Samurai Sally" from showing my ass with it in times past at certain parties. So when I hear Seth start mumbling something, I yell, "If you don't shut the fuck up, I'm gonna come in there with that sword!"

He got his stuff together and left. I never seen him again.

A few weeks later, my mother said, "You remember that big ol' tall boy that used to live over there with you?"

"What big ol' tall boy?"

"You know. That big ol' bald-headed boy. The one that drove that ugly ol' Thunderbird with the side window beat out of it." She had been over here and had met Seth on a number of occasions.

"Oh yeah. What about him?" I still had a bad taste in my mouth about him.

"Do you know the other day I saw him on *America's Most Wanted*? He is wanted for murder in Tennessee."

"What?!"

Well, I never found out if there was any truth to it. But my mother had met Seth enough times, and she's got a memory like an elephant. And she swore to God that she had seen him on *America's Most Wanted* and that bandit had strung off to Tennessee and killed somebody.

"It might be possible," I said. "He did rob Beau."

So I don't know about that. But I do know that he was very aggressive. He pushed his size around a lot. I knew when I came home that night from Beau's that I had better be prepared, because he might very well kick my ass. But the six bottles of wine had made up my mind that he was gonna have to give it a damned good shot. And he knew about that sword.

Seth happened to be there the night I earned my nickname.

A group of us used to get together, usually every Sunday evening, to drink and play spades. There'd be ten or twelve GIs and me. Just the regular crowd at that time, the current models and their buddies. And this particular night they happened to bring a new one. Now, before they brought anybody new over, the guys always told him, "Look, Dink's gay, so expect to hear some things, and don't be thrown off by anything he says to you." So he was well warned.

I don't remember exactly what it was I said that so upset this young man. It may have been something like, "You know, you got pretty lips." And I may have only said it just to see how he would react. I have been known to start a little shit just to get the guys going. I do recall that he had had a few too many drinks too.

He said to me, "If you say anything else like that again I'm gonna knock your face off."

The whole room got quiet. I looked at him and said, "You hold that fuckin' thought. I'll be right back." And I went to the bedroom and got that sword, and came back in the room yelling, "I'm gonna chop you up, motherfucker!"

I went to swinging toward his chair. He jumped out of the way. I whacked that chair three times. It was one of those old cheap pine wood chairs with the little poles on the back about an inch around. I came down on that thing and chopped it up pretty good. He had on some of those surfer shoes with the rubber bottoms, and one of them came off as he ran out the door. I ran out after him.

There was a twenty-four-hour store across the street. The people over there had become accustomed to getting free shows watching my place. And now here I was running down the side of the road in front of this BP station, yelling and waving this sword. But the kid was gone.

All the guys were out on the lawn. They were like, "Dink! You better put that sword away and get in the house before the cops come!"

"Well, y'all better go find that guy," I said. "There's his fuckin' shoe."

They went and found him. He had pulled his truck to the side of the road and he was hiding in the back of it. They came back and told me, "Dink, that boy said he ain't comin' back in here."

"Well, I don't blame him," I said. "You better take him back to the barracks."

So a couple of them took him back to the barracks and we went back to playing cards. And the sword went back in the bedroom and everything was fine. . . .

I was wild back then. I was a lot like those guys.

☆5☆ The Trouble with Harry

Gayle Martin

Most of the year I go hunting for Camp Pendleton Marines about once or twice a month, but come summer I tend to ramp up my visits to weekly or even two times a week. I usually head down on a Friday or Saturday night and look for an interesting Marine to bring back to Los Angeles with me.

I've found that on weekends Marines are usually loath to spend any time at all in their barracks if they can avoid it, so getting one to agree to make the ninety-minute trip to LA is easier than you might imagine. They don't always end up staying the entire weekend. Whether they get a ride back to Pendleton is entirely dependent upon their performance and attitude. A bad lay and poor manners gets them a ride to Union Station downtown where they can catch Amtrak back to Oceanside because I've suddenly remembered some pressing business that needs attending. Of course, driving back down to O'side sometimes presents an opportunity to hook up with a new Marine.

This particular morning after happened to be a Sunday. By the time I'd dropped off the latest Marine, it was early afternoon. I checked out the Crusty Spur, my usual haunt, and found it nearly empty with not a Marine to be seen. I don't really like prowling during the day. It was sunny and hot. The beach seemed like a good place to linger awhile before returning north.

Right next to the Oceanside pier is a small open-air amphitheater. I decided to kick back on one of the bleacher seats that faces the ocean. After about twenty minutes or so, a lone Marine came along and took a seat in one of the lower rows. From a distance he looked like he might be cute, so I pulled out a cigarette and went over to ask him for a light.

Unfortunately he turned out to be a German who had joined the Marine Corps in order to get his American citizenship. My interest cooled immediately. It's not that I don't find foreign accents appealing, but if I've got my heart set on a true-blue Marine, obviously only one who is American is going to do. So after making a couple of minutes of polite conversation, I took my leave and walked back up onto Pier View Way, back to where my car was parked outside the Spur.

I honestly had it in mind to just go home. It was Sunday, after all. I had to work the next day. And it was clearly going to be slim pickings as the only Marines I saw were running around getting their weekly regulation haircuts and picking up their freshly pressed uniforms from the various cleaners around town before heading back to base. I took one last peek into the bar. It was still nearly deserted. There were only four people inside. But one of them was a Marine.

Since it was such a long drive back I decided that one drink wouldn't hurt.

I took a seat at the bar and watched the Marine play pool with a longhaired biker type. It wasn't a very serious game of pool. They were just whacking the balls around the table. After they finished, the Marine came up, took the bar stool right next to me, and said, "Hey, what are you up to?" And that's how Gayle met Harry.

I told him I was just having a beer before heading back to Los Angeles. Harry asked me if I wanted to go to a party instead. He and his buddy had a keg they needed to finish off so they could return it to the liquor store and collect their deposit.

"Want to come help us drain it?"

I can't say it was an immediate decision on my part. I looked him over. He wasn't bad-looking, but kind of scruffy and a little too thin for my taste. I like my Marines to really look the part: clean-shaven, nice high-and-tight haircuts, and big, beefy builds. Harry was wearing glasses, his face was unshaven, and his dark blond hair looked like it hadn't been cut in weeks. It took some convincing to get me to come along, but convince me he did. Harry wasn't going to take no for an answer. While his physical appearance alone was not enough to sway me, the force of his personality more than did the job.

Have you ever had the feeling that your present course of action would prove to be a terrible mistake, yet found yourself somehow incapable of turning around and walking away? That's the feeling that overtook me as I left the Crusty Spur with Harry and his biker buddy.

I asked them if we should take my car, but Harry said no. There were a few other people they wanted to invite, and we went in search of them. He was like the Pied Piper. We just kept collecting scruffy misfits—none of whom were Marines—until there were about eight of us. I had no idea where the hell we were or where we were going. We just kept walking. I fucking hate walking!

I kept whining, "Why don't we just get my car?" "Why didn't we take my car?" "Where are we going?" "I think I'm just gonna go back to the Spur and head home."

And Harry just kept goading me on with him. "No, no, it's not much farther. Only one more stop. Let's have some fun. Why do you want to leave?"

Finally we ended up at this house on some dingy side street. There were already a few guys hanging out on the porch when we got there and at least three motorcycles parked in front. The keg was on the lawn and there was an assortment of patio furniture in various states of disrepair strewn about. I was the only chick there. This always makes me nervous. But Harry assured me, "Everyone's cool, these are my friends." And in reality in turned out to be Harry who I should have been concerned about, not the biker gang.

I think the beer in the keg was Budweiser. It always is, isn't it? I fucking hate Bud. It tastes like piss. Bud is *swill*. Why can't Marines drink a strong beer like Bass? Obviously I wasn't much help chugging down that keg. In fact, I took every opportunity to excuse myself to the bathroom and just pour whatever was in my cup down the sink. So I can't blame what ensued on being drunk, because I wasn't.

Harry kept up his relentless pursuit of me. Really, it wasn't that hard though. It's not like I'm *not* a total slut. He was a Marine. He told me he was a sergeant. He said he was all scruffy because he'd been out in the field for two weeks and just hadn't had a chance to get a haircut yet.

"You really need a shave," I said.

"I need a razor!" he immediately announced to all assembled. "Anybody got a razor? I need a shave."

Amazingly enough, someone actually produced one of those cheap disposable razors. Harry took it and came over and placed it in my hand.

"Go ahead and give me a shave."

I just looked at him. "Am I supposed to shave your face *dry?*"

He took back the razor, dipped it into his beer, and said, "Here, use this."

"You want me to shave you with *beer?*"

He laughed and took off his glasses. "Sure. You want me shaved, so shave me."

I took the razor and the beer, and took his face in my hands and started to shave him. It wasn't working though. The angle was all wrong. So I told him to turn around and lean back against me. The beer was on the table, and I held Harry's head with my left hand while I shaved with my right. I think I did a pretty good job of it too. I didn't cut him once, and by the time I finished he was looking a lot better to me. He was looking more like a Marine. I was starting to flirt now. We talked while I shaved and I told him I was going to massage school. With that revelation he of course requested a massage.

By this point I was well in the mood to play along. Harry was amusing and funny and getting better-looking every minute. We were having a good time. So once I finished with his face he took off his shirt and lay down on the grass. His biker buddies started hooting and hollering. One of them asked, "You gonna put on a sex show?"

"No," Harry told them, "Gayle's a professional masseuse. She's just giving me a massage."

It was the most half-assed massage I've ever given, but he seemed to like it. What he liked most was that while I was standing over him he managed to take a peek up my shorts and see that I wasn't wearing any underwear. Suddenly much more quiet and serious, he squinted up at me and said, "I like your undies."

"Like the color, huh?" I smirked at him.

With that, he snaked his hand up my leg and jammed two of his fingers straight into me. He didn't linger but pulled out his fingers and stuck them in his mouth.

I told him I really was not at all interested in putting on a sex show. But he assured me no one was paying any attention to us because they were busy drinking beer. It may have been true. I didn't really care. I just wanted his fingers back inside me. He quickly obliged.

"Do you want to go someplace?" I asked him. He suggested that since he didn't have to be at work until Tuesday he could come home with me. I told him that would be all right as long as he didn't mind taking the train back to Oceanside the next day.

It took us about three hours to get to Los Angeles. There wasn't any problem with traffic. Harry just decided that he needed to take me on a little detour first. It started at the San Onofre entrance to Camp Pendleton. When I stopped at the guard shack to show the MP my driver's license, Harry noticed some Boots waiting for the bus that runs through base to the "Outer Camps." Harry took it upon himself to offer them a ride. I didn't have any problem with this because I play taxi on Camp Pendleton all the time.

So the three "baby Marines," as I call them, piled into the backseat. I drove, and Harry talked. He repeated the same story to the Boots that he'd told me. He was a sergeant and he'd been in the Marine Corps about three years. That should have been a clue that something was awry. While it is entirely possible for a Marine to make sergeant that quickly, it's rare. If you're a pretty good Marine, you'll probably make corporal by the time your first four years are up.

But I pretty much just tuned out Harry's bluster to the gullible young Boots. We dropped them off at the School of Infantry and continued a bit farther down the road to Camp Horno. Harry jumped out of the car and ran inside the barracks to pack a bag. Next he directed me on a little tour of the beachfront property on base. It's actually a pretty sweet deal. Marines and their families can book a trailer right on the beach itself for about twenty-five dollars a night. There are bonfire pits and barbecue grills and the view is totally amazing. Harry told me that he'd book a trailer for the following weekend so I could bring my dogs down and spend the weekend on the beach with him. It struck me that I hadn't even had sex with him yet and he was already planning our future. I have to confess it sounded promising.

I like to tell myself that I'm interested only in having sex with Marines, nothing more. They are good-looking, have good bodies, and like to have fun. They always seem impressed that an older woman finds them interesting enough to actually listen to, let alone have sex with.

But the truth is that I would love to find something more.

And Marines do as much for my self-esteem as I do for theirs. They're easy to pick up, so I don't have to worry about rejection. There aren't many women around base or even around town, so I don't have much competition. And they're lonely and far from home so they'll spend hours and hours just talking and tell you everything about themselves, even their deepest secrets. They make me feel special and wanted, which makes me the perfect mark for the kind of guy who can figure out what it really is I'm looking for. Harry played my emotions like a virtuoso.

And the sex wasn't bad either.

After we left the base Harry spent most of the ride with his hand between my legs. By the time we got to Los Angeles I was as horny as I'd ever been in my life. No sooner were we in my apartment than my shorts were off and Harry's cock was inside me. It was thick and meaty and I watched it slide in and out of me as Harry held my legs in the air standing next to the bed so he could pump me good and hard. He hadn't bothered to take off his clothes so his jeans were pooled around his knees. He was slamming into me so hard that I could hear his balls slapping against my butt with each forward thrust. We both came fast and hard.

My dogs were going crazy in the other room so I quickly got into a pair of pants and took them for a walk. Harry came with me.

My dogs loved Harry more than anyone they'd ever met. They were crazy about him and had no inkling that he would turn out to be a lying, cheating, manipulative piece of shit. Never trust a dog's judgment. Their good favor is too easily bought with belly rubs and treats.

My good favor is easily bought with exceptionally good sex and Harry proceeded to provide that in spades. As soon as we were back from dog walking, we were back in bed fucking our brains out. I have to give him that; he was a really great fuck. He may not have been the best-looking Marine I'd ever had in my bed, but he definitely knew what he was doing there and he had loads of fun doing it.

He also had a great cock. It was the kind of cock I really like to wrap my lips around, nice and fat and long, but not so long that I couldn't take the whole thing into my mouth or ever felt like I was being skewered on it. And he had incredible stamina, which is something I consider critical, as I don't tire easily.

We spent hours in bed that Sunday night and by the time we called a time out I was already offering to give him a ride back to base on Monday night so he could stay all day Monday. I had to go into work, but it wasn't going to be all day and I figured we could spend several more hours screwing before I took him home. That was cool by Harry. We fell asleep wrapped around each other and woke up during the night and had sex again. When morning rolled around I woke up to his face between my legs and a couple of orgasms before breakfast.

I had no qualms about leaving Harry in my apartment while I went to the office for five hours. He told me he'd take the dogs out for me so I even left him my house key. When I got home I found Harry ensconced on the couch watching television with the dogs curled up with him and a twelve-pack of beer on the coffee table. A mostly depleted twelve-pack. I was a little put out when I noticed that also on the table was a nearly empty bottle of 1800 Cuervo Tequila. It had been in my kitchen cupboard and nearly full when I'd left. I always have lots of quality alcohol around, but it usually lasts me a long time. I'm a slut but not a lush.

Harry noticed my eye on the bottle. "We can go shopping tonight. I'll buy you some groceries and we'll get more tequila."

"I don't think we'll have time for that," I said. "I need to get you back to base and I don't want to be out too late."

"Oh yeah, well, I called my commanding officer and I don't have to go back until Wednesday."

"You're kidding." I just looked at him. Nice of him to run it past me first.

"No, no, I have a lot of leave I need to use up. You don't mind, right?"

Yes, I minded. It's not like *I* had lots of leave I needed to use up, and to tell the truth I like my alone time. I also don't care much for surprises. Harry was lots of fun, but I was expecting him to leave.

I didn't say any of that, of course. I should have, but I didn't.

When I came home from work Tuesday, Harry told me he'd gotten the rest of the week off, and I did start to wonder a little. But even then I really didn't question it that much. I quickly accepted the fact that he was going to stay. After all, I was enjoying myself. His cooking was nearly as good as the sex. Every night he made dinner for us. It was usually steak and it was the best damn steak I ever had. He told me his parents owned a steakhouse in Detroit. They were wealthy and apparently also quite generous. Everything Harry bought—from the groceries to the copious quantities of alcohol to the gas he put in my car—he paid for with his father's credit card.

I ended up taking Thursday and Friday off work, even though I couldn't really afford to. Thursday we went to a local firing range. Harry wanted to teach me how to shoot. Even though he wasn't able to show me anything I didn't already know how to do, we still had fun. Friday he announced that my car "looked like ass" and that he would wash it for me. So I gave him the keys. He was gone for hours, but when he got back my car looked like it was brand new.

Saturday morning he asked if he could borrow my car for a few hours because he had to check in at base. I let him. By 10 p.m. I was more than a little annoyed that he wasn't back yet. Around 11 p.m. I got a phone call from him informing me that he had checked into a motel room in San Clemente because he was too drunk to drive back to LA.

I went completely ballistic and called a friend of mine who was kind enough to drive me all the way down there to get my car.

But oh, what an easily swayed fucking nitwit I was! When I got to San Clemente Harry was all apologies and caresses and nibbles and licks and "Come on, why don't you just stay tonight and go home in the morning?" So I stayed. He bought me dinner at the diner next door. We had sex, but it was less amazing than usual because Harry was still pretty drunk. In the morning I left without waking him up or saying good-bye. This was Sunday.

That night he called and told me that he'd been at work all day long, but that he would love to see me if I wanted to come down. He had kept the room at the motel for us. He even asked me to bring the dogs. So I did. When I arrived Harry told me he'd missed me a lot even though it had been only one day. Then he said, "I'm falling in love with you."

"I love you too!" I blurted.

"I want you to marry me."

Yes, believe it or not, he actually suggested that we go to Vegas and get married.

Oops! I was already married. I'd been separated for two years, but I didn't tell him that. I just said that it was too early for him to be talking about marriage when we'd practically just met. To this day I thank Christ my ex-husband and I were too damn lazy to do the paperwork. If I hadn't been married already I most likely would have agreed to go to Vegas and marry Harry.

I called in sick and stayed down in San Clemente that Monday while Harry went to work. Once he got back he told me he'd gotten the rest of the week off and offered that if I didn't want him at my place he would just stay at the motel. Of course I took him back to Los Angeles with me where he spent the rest of that week screwing my brains out, drinking all my liquor and the countless cases of beer he bought, and asking me over and over again to please marry him. At moments I briefly toyed with the idea of committing bigamy, but in some inexplicable access of sanity I kept saying no.

At the end of the week he suddenly announced he was going to go visit his parents in Detroit. He asked me to come with him, but there was simply no way I could take off any more time from work. I dropped him off at the Amtrak station and tearfully said good-bye.

Two days later he called me from Detroit, drunk and crying, telling me how much he missed me and how much he loved me and that he'd told his parents all about me and we should get married and he was going to bring me an engagement ring, blah blah blah. This kept up for about four or five days—phone calls every night with professions of his undying love.

Then one night I didn't get a call. I didn't think that much of it, but I missed hearing from him. When another day went by, however, I called Detroit and spoke to Harry's mother. She told me that he'd left to go back to LA the day before. That seemed weird. Why hadn't Harry called to let me know he was coming back?

After another four days went by and I still didn't hear a word, I was well and truly pissed. Just when I had all but written Harry off completely, lo and behold he called me from Union Station, looking for a ride. I went and got him. He had a fresh regulation haircut and a twelve-pack of beer in his luggage. I was so pissed I barely spoke to him except to ask where the hell he'd been and why hadn't he called. Once again, he had all his apologies in order. He explained that he'd been on base and hadn't had a chance to call because he'd been so busy.

Something just felt off. I wasn't sure what it was, and I didn't even know why I thought there was something funny going on. Having those few days to stew in my anger must have brought me back to my senses enough that I finally started to actually think about everything he told me. How in the hell does someone in the military get nearly three weeks' vacation with no notice at all? I've dated military guys before and that's just not how it works. A lot of them get their leave postponed again and again. On that ride back to my place I finally asked the question: "Are you absent without leave?"

"No, no!"

Harry said that his four-year stint was nearly up and he had all this leave he needed to take and so they were letting him take it.

"How much leave?"

"About three months."

"Harry, you can tell me if you're UA [Unauthorized Absence], I really don't care."

Once again he assured me he was legally on vacation. But I just wasn't buying it. Somehow I suddenly stopped buying everything he'd told me. It was as if the brain fog had lifted. I knew without any doubt that he was lying. I just needed to prove it.

Knowing he was a liar didn't stop me from having sex with him when we got back to my place. But it wasn't the same. I hate liars. He kept insisting that everything was fine. And he also kept insisting on trying to fuck me in the ass. He had never before suggested anal sex. This wasn't something I'd normally necessarily be disinclined to do, but my sense of fun had evaporated. The feel of his fingers and then his cock trying to push at my asshole was making me irritable, uncomfortable, and confused. I felt like he was trying to pull something over on me.

I wanted to get rid of him but didn't quite know how.

The next day I had my opportunity. He asked to borrow my car for a few hours, and I went ahead and gave him the keys. As soon as he left I started rummaging through his bags. Even though I had no idea exactly what I was looking for, as soon as I found it I knew it was what I'd been expecting to find. A marriage certificate. Dated the day before. Harry had married some girl. In Las Vegas. Yesterday.

I just stared at it. I was fucking stupefied, but at the same time pleased that I was right.

I continued searching his bags until I found a hotel receipt with a list of phone calls. My number wasn't on it, but there were a couple of others with southern California area codes so I called one of them and asked for the girl whose name was on the marriage certificate. I got her on the first try.

"Hi, Rosie. My name is Gayle. I was wondering if you could tell me what your husband is doing here in Los Angeles with me?"

I know it was mean, springing it on her like that, but that's the mood I was in.

Rosie was just as flabbergasted as I had been and asked me who the hell I was. When she regained control, she said, "I need to see you."

I told her that she was welcome to come to LA but that she'd probably want to get on the road immediately so that she'd get here before Harry got back to my apartment, as I would really like to surprise him. I gave her directions and told her to be sure not to park on my street so that Harry wouldn't see her car.

She was a stupid fucking twit and parked on my street. So we lost the surprise factor. But I did manage to get quite a bit of information from her before Harry got there. Turns out the reason Harry was so keen on getting my car washed is that day he drove it to see Rosie. He told her he'd bought the car. I looked at her like she was a total idiot and said, "Didn't you notice the New York plates?"

Well, yes, she had noticed the plates, but Harry had some story for that too. And it turns out that all the days he was in LA with me, Rosie thought he was on base working. And vice versa. That day that I called in sick so that I could hang around all afternoon in a motel room in San Clemente? Yep, he was with her. We'd both been had.

Harry was ready for us. When he came in the door he didn't even act concerned or apologetic.

"I guess I'm busted. Where's my wife?"

Then he actually kicked one of my dogs out of his way as he went to grab Rosie out of the bathroom where she'd run and hid. I would have fucking belted him one at that point had I not been so shocked that the fucker had kicked one of my dogs after they'd loved him so much.

When he brought Rosie back into the living room the screaming started. We were both yelling at him. All he had to say to us was, "I'm in love with both of you. I just couldn't decide which one I wanted."

"So you just decided that you'd fool us both?" I asked. His response was a shrug. I could really kick myself that I didn't throw him out right then and there. I should have thrown them both out the door and said good riddance. But I didn't. Even though I knew he'd been lying to me, there was still some part of me that ached to believe I meant something to him and that he wasn't just using me. So instead I said, "You need to decide right now. If you want to stay with me, then you can get an annulment and Rosie can leave. If you want to stay with her, then you can leave with her right now."

Rosie was obviously just as dumb as me because instead of storming out the door alone she waited for an answer. Storming out the door is, however, what she ended up doing as Harry announced that he preferred to stay with me.

After she was gone Harry and I just stood there and stared at each other. Then finally his apologies started rolling and for a little while I again let them sway me. I started crying and told him how much he'd hurt my feelings and how could I ever trust him again and more pathetic crap like that. We sat around the house for a few hours watching television before I suddenly came to my senses and told him he needed to get the hell out. He assented without protest and asked me if I would take him to a hotel.

"Fine, which one?"

"The Century Plaza."

If you've never heard of it, it's one of those very posh hotels that movie stars stay at. A standard room costs several hundred dollars a night. As usual, Harry put it on his dad's credit card. When we got to the hotel, I was all set to just take off, but he begged me to come inside and have a drink and maybe dinner.

I went up to his room with him and we drank. But when he attempted to convince me to have sex with him I told him he was an asshole for even thinking about any sex with me before he got an annulment. On my way out he begged me to call him the next day and told me he really loved me and promised he'd get an annulment as soon as possible. I went home and cried myself to sleep.

The next night I called the hotel. Rosie answered and told me Harry didn't want to talk to me. Five minutes later my phone rang. It was Harry. I had had enough. I hung up on him and called his mother in Detroit.

She too had a story for me.

As it turns out, Harry's parents really do own a restaurant, but they aren't exactly among Detroit's wealthiest. Harry had charged nearly $10,000 on his father's credit card within the past month and they'd only just now found out about it after the bank called them to ask if all the charges were legitimate. Harry's mom told me she'd canceled the credit card. She also told me that this was the third time Harry had gone AWOL, and that he was only a private because he'd been busted down in rank at least twice for dereliction of duty. She suggested that I call the Marine Corps and tell them where he was hiding.

I took her advice. The military police were very interested in what I had to say, and the first thing they asked me was whether I'd had sex with Harry after he'd gotten married. Like an idiot, I covered for him and said no. He was going to be in enough trouble as it was. I told them where he was.

I wish I could have been there when they picked him up. The look on his face might have made up for some of the trouble and heartache he caused me. But as it turned out I just had to content myself with the knowledge that as a result of my phone call he went from the Century Plaza to the brig. Fucker.

☆6☆

Barracks Bad Boys & Samurai Sally III: Kyle 'n Shooter

Dink Flamingo

Shooter came to me through another model with whom he had joined the Army on the buddy system. I had already met the buddy and done some work with him. One night he brought Shooter over. We went upstairs and shot the video. And Shooter was really excited about it. He was really into doing what he was doing. And when he shot his load . . . He was sitting on the infamous old blue-and-white striped couch that can be seen in most of my very early tapes. He blew his load over his shoulder and it hit the wall. When we came out of the bedroom and went back downstairs, his buddy asked, "How'd he do?" From that moment on his name was Shooter. And that's still what he goes by today.

Afterward we all decided that we were going to party our asses off at this bar in a college town just north of here. I wound up getting kicked out of the club and passing out in the back of Shooter's 1964 Cadillac Eldorado, a big ol' rusted-out piece of shit convertible. They brought me back home and I pulled one of my Dink routines. I refused to get out of the car. I distinctly remember Shooter saying, "Who the fuck *is* this guy, man? *Get him* out of my car!" Finally I got out of the car, and I was standing on the side of the road taking this big piss. Shooter just shook his head, but he was laughing too. He said, "You know, you gotta love this fuckin' guy. He won't get out of your fuckin' car, and then he pisses in his own front yard!" From that point on we were extremely good friends.

Shooter really thought I was a character. He had never met anybody quite like me, anybody who just didn't give a fuck like I did. So he and I got to be real close. And he started bringing a nonstop buffet of soldiers over to my house. What he would tell them in the barracks was, "You gotta meet this Dink dude, man. You're not gonna believe this guy. He is fuckin' crazy!" For all the new guys that came into his unit, it became standard procedure for them to be whisked away to Dink's, and hopefully have their minds blown before the evening was over.

Now, I don't know this to be a fact, but I often suspected that Shooter brought over the soldiers whom he personally was attracted to. Just to see what I could get them to do. And one such soldier was Kyle.

I fell absolutely in love with this boy the very moment I set eyes on him. Oh, he was beautiful. He had greenish eyes—almost tiger eyes. The straightest smile you'd ever seen. High cheekbones. Beautiful skin. And he had the most beautiful color hair. Very, very soft brown. Of course he had the typical GI haircut, but Kyle was a bit rebellious. He refused to cut his bangs. He would gel it down when he was at work. But when he was out and about off duty his bangs would fall down his forehead almost in his eyes.

Kyle was just stunning. He was one of those people who, when he walked into a crowded room, just commanded everybody's attention, no matter who else was there. And it wasn't because he was loud or boisterous; it was because he was beautiful. And it didn't matter who or what you were. Even the boys who I considered the straightest I often seen radiate toward Kyle because his beauty was . . . angelic.

He was six foot one, about one eighty-five. Very well defined, and very smooth. And his ass . . . To this day I have never seen an ass quite as beautiful as Kyle's. At parties all the boys used to pick on him and say, "Dude! You've got an ass like a woman! Can I feel your ass? I wanna fuck it, man!"

Anyway, when Shooter brought this kid over and we went to lunch it quickly became pretty obvious that Kyle had heard all the talk at the barracks about me.

Now, what I didn't come to find out until later was that previous to coming into the Army Kyle had had some problems. He had rebelled at home and had left his family in Oregon. And eventually he found himself somewhere in the streets of Seattle, where for a short time he got involved in the heroin scene. Then he found Jesus, and somehow through his newfound faith was able to pull himself out of that and realize that he had to do something with his life, and he didn't know what to do so he joined the Army. So by the time he got through basic training, and got here, he had strengthened himself by studying the Bible with evangelical fervor. And when he came to meet me that day, he had it in his head that he was going to bring me out of the life of iniquity I was living.

But what Kyle couldn't know about me was that I had already gone through a very similar period in my own life several years earlier. I had been exactly where he was. I wasn't involved in heroin, but I'd gone through the same thing with religion. And I don't mean to discount religion, because it works for a lot of people. But for a lot of people it's also something to hide behind, and a way to hide what they consider personal shortcomings.

At lunch he told me how I needed to find Jesus Christ and accept Him as my personal savior. And he cited Bible verses condemning homosexuality.

After he was done with everything he had to say, I told him, "You know, if you're going to be a preacher, you need to learn how to preach."

"What do you mean?"

"If you're gonna be an effective preacher, you need to preach something that people want to hear. People don't want to hear hate. And they don't want to hear how wrong they are, and how much they're failing as human beings. They wanna hear about love." I said, "If I've learned anything about God, the one thing I've learned is that God is *love*."

That kind of sacked him. It blew him away. He did not know how to respond to that. Suddenly his way of bringing about the power of Jesus Christ had been challenged by something as simple as that four letter word. I remember him being quite taken aback. And looking almost bitterly defeated for the rest of lunch.

And Shooter was just laughing and laughing. He thought it was the funniest thing, that Kyle had run himself into a corner. Which of course only made poor Kyle sink even deeper into his chair.

But at that point I felt pretty disgusted. Even though the whole time he was talking I could see things about him. I could see things in his eyes that made me suspect that at the right time he could probably suck the chrome off a trailer hitch. But obviously he was going through a lot of stuff right then. And I thought, *I really don't have time to waste with a twenty-year-old self-proclaimed minister. As beautiful as he is, as much as I would just love to eat his ass, it's going to be a while before I have him for dessert.* So I paid the bill and left the two of them there at the restaurant.

☆ ☆ ☆

Later that night I was at home. I had decided that I wasn't going to do anything that night. There were a lot of messages on the answering machine, but I just ignored them.

A knock came at the door. I got up, went to the door, and it was . . . Kyle. And I looked behind him because I expected to see Shooter. And there was no Shooter.

I let him in. "You want something to drink?"

"Sure. What do you got?"

I named off some nonalcoholic beverages.

"Do you have anything with alcohol?"

I thought, *Hmmm. Has the preacher left his Bible at the barracks and gone out for a nightcap?*

So I fixed him a drink and we sat down and started talking. I was dancing around the issue of why he was there. I was going to let him tell me why.

Kyle said to me, "Is it true what I hear?"

"Well, it probably is. What did you hear?"

"I hear you shave a really good ass."

You see, at that time I was doing a lot of shaving of the guys. It was another thing that Shooter would bring them over for. He would bring them over for me to shave their balls and their assholes. Because it was really just coming in fashion then that everybody wanted to shave their balls and trim their pubes. And I had come to be known as "the dick, ass, and balls barber of base." I had affectionately won that title and I was very proud of it, actually.

Kyle commenced to hinting around that he would like for me to shave his ass. So I took him to the bedroom, and I opened up a drawer full of porn. "You can choose whatever you want out of here."

A few minutes later I was in the bathroom. I was running warm water in a bowl, getting the shaving cream and razor ready, when I heard him say, "Holy shit!" I just kind of laughed to myself: *I guess he's found one of my gay videos.*

I came back in. "What is it?"

"These guys! They're fucking!"

"Uh, yeah . . ."

Kyle was simply amazed. He had never seen anything like this before. Then he said, "Hey, wait a minute. That's this bedroom. That's this bed!"

"Yeah," I said. "I shot that."

"You *know* these guys?"

"No, I just let them borrow my house. Yes, I know 'em."

"They're here? At post? No way. No fuckin' way, man! Oh, that is so sick."

I went back to the kitchen. Just to see if he would get up and snatch the tape out. I waited and I listened and I did not hear the tape popping out. I came back, and he was completely naked. Lying there with his hard dick just sticking straight up over his belly. Staring at the video. I didn't offer to take the tape out, and he didn't ask me to either.

"My God . . . I can't believe this."

"Well, you're not dreaming." And I actually went over and gave him a little pinch. "Come on, let's get you on up so I can shave your ass."

So I positioned him to where he was up on his hands and knees, arching his back, and I was standing behind him. Because he's a taller fellow. And I just started taking a lot of shaving cream and just rubbing it all over his ass, rubbing it between his cheeks. More than his ass needed. A lot more. And trying not to laugh, because here this guy came over with the excuse of me shaving his asshole, and he's virtually smooth!

But I was playing right on into it. I was rubbing his ass like I was shaving a huge full beard. And I went down and start rubbing his balls, because I was gonna shave his balls too. His dick was still hard as a brick. And in a split second I reached underneath and grabbed his dick and stroked it with the shaving cream. A little stream of precum came down and hit the bed, and it just hung there. And I thought that was the most beautiful thing.

But I was trying not get too carried away. I wanted to act as if I had some sort of self-discipline and restraint, or whatever. I just continued on with the job at hand, being the barber. Until I finished shaving his ass—slicker than it already was. Then I did go back to stroking his dick. Streams of precum just started pouring out of his dick.

So I was playing with him. I started eating his ass. I just buried my face right in, shaving cream and all. While I had my hand on his cock—givin' him "a rusty trombone," is what I heard one boy call it, when you're eating somebody's ass and jerking him off at the same time. I had tasted so much shaving cream before I wasn't affected by it. I was just bound and determined to get my tongue as far up his ass as I could. And I did. And he was loving it. Suddenly he flipped over.

At that point he pretty much gave me the signal that it was all a go. And it was great. I serviced him, and then at his request I came on him.

☆☆☆

Kyle became a frequent visitor to my house. But he always held the position that he was not like the others, that he was different. And he was. He was very different. It was almost as if he were an officer, in the whole group.

We became very, very close friends. Well, quite simply, I was head over heels in love with him. But I didn't express it a lot. I made a point not to do so. Although it was very obvious, and I know he knew it. But I tried very hard to treat him just like the rest of them. The only time I think I did show favoritism is when we were alone. I would do things for him that I wouldn't do for the others. Let him stay for long periods of time. Cook for him.

I have never been a so-called military mother by any means. If they want their uniforms pressed or something they had better take them to the fucking cleaners, because I'm not into that. But for Kyle I would do things. Because I sensed that he needed something like that.

Sexually things were kind of one-sided for the most part. Which I didn't necessarily mind. But he did make an effort on quite a number of occasions to do more and to be more involved. But I knew that he harbored a lot of guilt after each session. After one of the first few times he went back to the barracks and told Shooter, "Oh my God. I let him eat my *asshole.* I cannot do that anymore. I cannot go back over there!" And then he would keep coming over. But even after he had been coming over for two years he still had a lot of problems with it. Which is why I never pushed anything. I always let things happen the way he wanted them to.

Obviously, after that first time he couldn't immediately come back and ask to have his ass shaved again. He usually started out with the excuse of needing a back rub, and of course the back rub would turn into sex. That was always the standard fare with him. Never could he come out and say, "Can you service me?" or "Can we have sex?" He could never do that. It always had to start out in some indirect way.

One year the boys threw a big birthday party for me. At some point Kyle had someone take him somewhere, and came back and went straight into the bathroom. Now, this happened in a house full of GIs. There must have been twenty-five of them there. It was mixed company, too. A lot of them were guys that Kyle did not know. And he came out of the bathroom dressed in a Chippendale-style dancer outfit, with the little tuxedo neck thing that straps on with Velcro, the Velcro tuxedo arm cuffs, and the G-string with the little tuxedo-looking thing in the front.

He sat on my lap in this getup. He said, "I'm going to be your personal server for tonight."

"Great."

And so he followed me around the entire night. After the party was over, after the crowd was gone (except for Shooter, of course; Shooter always passed out, and he always made sure that he had a couple of boys pass out with him), Kyle and I were both pretty fucked up.

He said, "You want to come in here and help me take this thing off?"

I thought, *What do you need help with? It's Velcro, come on.* But I said, "Okay. Sure."

So I went in the bedroom and I helped him take off this little getup that he'd worn for me the entire night. Because he always needed some kind of unspoken transition to sexual contact.

One night about two years into my relationship with Kyle, Shooter convinced a group of the guys to go down to one of the bigger cities to a gay club. Now, a lot of the crazier soldiers, as straight and as butch as they are, have no problems going to some gay bar or doing even wilder things. There was one boy from West Virginia, for example, known as "Leatherhead." His last name sounded very similar to that, and his face looked like leather. He was one of the ugliest people I'd ever seen in my life. He was in the same platoon as Kyle and Shooter. They were at a briefing, and it was almost Halloween. And an officer at this briefing looked at Leatherhead and said, "Goddamn, boy! You've already got your fuckin' costume for Halloween! Fuck," he said, "you're Frankenstein!" And he did; he looked exactly like Frankenstein without the bolts in his head. Ugly, ugly kid. But just sweet as could be, and very likeable, and a whole lot of fun to party with.

Well, Leatherhead would go with Shooter down to these gay clubs. And oh, he thought it was a high time to hook up with what he considered a hot transvestite. He'd come back and tell the story, and have no problem telling you that "she" had had a bigger dick than he did.

Kyle, on the other hand, would not partake in such adventures. If the boys wound up at someplace like that, he would sit in the car. He wouldn't go in. Shooter would beg him, "Please come in."

"No. I'm not going in there, and I wish you guys would leave. I don't want to be here."

Well, on one of those trips, while he was sitting out in the car waiting for the boys to have their fun, Kyle got ahold of some cocaine. Evidently some drug dealer came by the parking lot and Kyle made a buy. While he was waiting for his buddies he snorted this cocaine. And the next day the unit had a piss test. And Kyle came up "hot."

Now here's somebody who loved the Army. Kyle had been an exemplary soldier. He was a platoon leader. He took his job very seriously. He really loved what he was doing. And as soon as that happened, everything instantly changed.

He had moved into my house and was living in one of the downstairs bedrooms at this time. And everything was going really well. One night of making a mistake turned everything in his life upside down.

He came home from extra duty one day and said, "I'm leaving."

"What, are you moving back into the barracks?"

"No. I'm going AWOL," he said. "I just can't do it anymore, Dink. I just can't. I hate the Army now. I'm fucked. I'm never gonna be able to regain my rank. I'll never be able to be a platoon leader again."

I said, "Well, of course you will. You just got to work through this."

"No. I'm leaving."

"Well, you can still stay here."

Of course I started thinking back to Rob. And I said to myself, *Oh God, I don't wanna go through this again.* But I'd made my mind up that if he needed to be there, that's where he was going to be.

About three days later he came in and said, "Dink, everybody in the barracks knows I'm over here. I'm afraid that they're going to come over here, and that you're going to get into some kind of trouble because I'm here. I don't want that to happen. So I'm gonna leave. I'm going back to Oregon."

He had talked to his mom. His mother and father were divorced. He didn't get along with either of them very well. And of course the current happenings weren't helping those relationships at all. So he didn't have anybody that he could ask for anything.

"Can you just give me enough money to get to Oregon?" he asked. "As soon as I get there, I can find me a job."

"Of course I will." And I gave him what we thought was enough.

I'll never forget standing out in the yard that day, hugging him good-bye. Both of us were crying. I did not want to see him go. I really didn't. But at the same time I appreciated him not wanting any heat to come down on me. That meant a lot to me.

So he left, and he made it as far as Colorado. He called me up. "Man! The goddamn transmission—"

I said "What?!" Because that wasn't like him, to use God's name in vain.

He took a breath and said, "The God-durn transmission fell out of my car. I'm stuck in Parachute fuckin' Colorado. But guess what?"

"What?"

"I've got a job already. I met this lady that owns this small hotel; it's about twenty rooms. She's willing to let me stay there for free in exchange for doing maintenance around the place."

And he was really upbeat.

Well, Kyle stayed in Parachute. And got an even better job as a night manager of a large grocery store. He was doing extremely well, and he was very happy. Until his bitch of a mother decided that it would be best if he were back in Oregon under her control. She called the post here and told them where to find him. A couple of nights later when he came into work they were there waiting to arrest him. He called me from Fort Knox, Kentucky, after he'd outprocessed.

"I don't know what to do," he said. "I don't have a job anymore. And I really like Parachute. I'd like to go back there. Right now I can't afford it. Can I come and stay with you for a little while?"

"Sure."

So I got him here, and he stayed a couple of weeks. I was happy to have him come back. We had a good time. And a lot of good conversations. But I could tell that he really did want to go back to Parachute. So I helped him get back there. And I helped him talk to his boss at the store. He ended up getting his job back. And a few months later he met a girl and married her.

They've been married for a couple of years now. Shooter jokes about the fact that they still don't have any children. "Dude. He don't even fuck her, man!"

Shooter says it's because he's gay.

"Dude, he's a homo, man! He just can't admit it. Come on, Dink! Don't you realize?"

"Yes, Shooter, and he's waiting for you to come and rescue him."

"Well, dude, I'm goin'! I'm gonna go out there and fuck him! And maybe his wife will watch, or somethin'."

But sometimes you really did have to wonder a little about Kyle. Because Kyle would sometimes do strange things. One time he went to get his car fixed at a local auto parts place. And when he came back he told us, "While I was watching the guy work on my car I went around the side of that building and jerked off. Just jerked off right there."

Shooter and I looked at each other, like, "Goddamn! He's more of a freak than we are!"

"Wait a minute," I said. "You *watched* the guy working on your car and you beat off."

"Yeah!" he said. "I came all over the side of the fuckin' building."

"*What* about that was erotic?"

"Oh, I don't know. I was thinkin' about something else."

I said, "The guy couldn't see you?"

"Well, he wasn't looking."

"Could he see you from where he was at?"

"Well, I'm sure he could if he looked."

So behind all his preaching, Kyle did have some interesting little hang-ups.

And it's funny because looking back now, I think that when he came over that first night to get shaved, he had not at all given up on winning me over to Christ. He'd just realized that if he were going to win, he was going to have to play the game a bit differently. But what a great example of a committed Christian—coming over and deciding to actually put his ass in someone's face to win him over to Christ.

Kyle was ultimately successful in some ways, though. Throughout our relationship there were times when I actually did get up on Sunday morning and go to church with him.

Shooter, on the other hand, never had any qualms about sex. In terms of being totally secure in his sexuality, hell, he was probably more secure in his sexuality than I was! Sex just was not a hang-up for him.

I consider Shooter a barracks bad boy even though he never got kicked out of the military. He pulled his time, got his honorable discharge. He was a good soldier. But while he was in the Army he was the *ringleader* of all these boys, always getting them doing something they had no business doing. He could get everybody in the barracks in trouble and not get in trouble himself. The boy was so lucky, it was like he was untouchable. He could do anything. I mean, at one point Shooter knocked two teeth out of his commanding officer's head and still did not get in trouble for it.

Shooter eventually got out of the Army and became a police officer.

He and I remain real close friends. We have conversations two or three times a week. And this is the funny thing about him now: He'll call me while he's on duty. He works in some small shit-pot town; it reminds me so much of a Barney Fife situation. He'll pull off on the side of the road somewhere and call me up.

I'll say, "What are you doin'?"

"I'm sittin' in the patrol car beatin' off."

"What?! What if they got a microphone in that thing or somethin'?"

"I don't give a fuck. Let 'em listen. I hope they get off on it too."

And some of the most enjoyable conversations I ever have is when he's sitting on the side of the road in Podunk, Indiana, talking to me about how he wishes I were there to suck his cock.

Shooter never classified himself as gay, straight, bi, or anything. He classified himself as a person that wanted to have a good time and he didn't care who he had it with, as long as it was fun and as long as it felt good.

He'd have sex with women. There was a lot of female involvement in the sex that he and I had. He would bring a female over, and she'd just be sort of a side piece. She'd wind up in bed with us and get neglected and ignored until he and I had our thing finished. Then I'd go off to sleep and he'd be on the other side of the bed, fucking the shit out of her.

Shooter was the most open, the most sexually comfortable person that I have ever met in my life. I mean, to the point that he is a person that understands what it means, I think, to be a man. And that our main goal as men, regardless of whatever we claim to be our agenda, is to *get off*.

And he has no hang-ups about it. Recently he called me up and said, "Dink, dude! You're not gonna fuckin' believe this, man. You can't fuckin' tell anybody!" Then he said, "I don't give a fuck if you tell 'em or not.

"I was at the store. I had just gotten off duty, and this old lady was outside the store. I went in, I bought a six-pack of beer, and I came back out. And this old-ass black lady—"

"What do you mean 'old'?"

"About sixty. She said, 'Let me have one of those beers!' I told her, 'Oh, you'll have to suck my dick for one of these.' And she says, 'Okay'! So I put the bitch in my car and brought her back to my apartment!"

"What? Are you fuckin' out of your mind?" I said. "How *old* was this woman?"

"Sixty! I told you, sixty!"

"And you let her suck your dick?"

"Hell yeah, dude! She sucked my dick for a beer!"

I could not believe this story.

"She looked kind of rough, dude."

"How rough?"

"Pretty fuckin' rough, man. We get back to the apartment, and it's hot as fuck. I turn on the fan, and it blows her dress up over her head. When I saw what was underneath, oh man! Dude! I was like, 'You gotta finish your beer. You gotta go.' But she wouldn't leave until she gave me the fuckin' blow job that she promised me for the beer."

"Why didn't you just tell her to get the fuck out?"

"Hell no! I let her suck my dick."

"Where did you come?"

"In her mouth."

"Well, did you take her back to the store?"

"No. I locked the door as soon as she walked out."

And this is just the kind of person Shooter is. As a matter of fact, I think a lot of times, his openness, his willingness to be open-minded, was inspiring for a lot of those other boys. He had that quality about him. And not because he was deceitful, not because he was calculating. But because he was bold and determined and did not worry what other people thought. And that in itself made him a leader. Those other boys would watch him, and they would be like, "Well, fuck, if Shooter can do it, so can I." And they would follow suit in all of the seedy and inappropriate things that the troops in this certain unit involved themselves in.

Which somehow or other I was always tied into too. His job was to get them off base and to get them to me, and to the house of iniquity, and from there we could work our magic.

He never asked for a finder's fee. He just wanted to be part of the action. He wanted to be part of what was going on.

So through it all, I would say Shooter was the baddest barracks bad boy I ever knew. And some of the best friends that I ever made were guys that I met through him.

He comes down to visit, and there'll be a whole new group of guys hanging around my house. He and I will go back to talking about the old days. About that group of twenty-five or so guys that he and Kyle were part of. And those really were, in a lot of ways, the glory days. That was the group.

These new guys will often feel sort of left out. They're like, "God, it sounds like a lot of fun. And now we're just sitting here listening about it."

One of the last few times that Shooter visited we were out on the deck, cooking steaks on the grill and having a lot of beers. Quite a good number of people were here. And one of the boys who had just started hanging out here began saying something about, "Oh yeah, I've been around here for a couple weeks now. I know what goes on."

Shooter was smoking a cigar, and just looked at him. And my friend Beau was there too, drunk on Glenlivet, grabbing each side of the bench he was sitting on, sort of holding himself up. He looked up over his spectacles.

After this kid was done bragging about how he was a veteran of all of two weeks, Shooter took a big puff of that cigar and said, "Boy, you don't know shit. Nothin' ever changes around Dink's place but the fucking clientele. And nobody stays for free."

☆7☆

What Are Friends For? (A Straight Soldier's Story)

Scott Moraz

In the mid-1990s, chat rooms became an easily accessible form of entertainment. With my newly purchased computer, I visited many of them while my wife worked evenings. With hopes of getting one to sign up, Internet services offered free online hours that I would spend seeking fun in the various chat rooms. Having fair typing skills and countless strangers available at my fingertips, I looked forward to instigating conversations with other people also in search of excitement. The "Lesbian Lounge," "Bisexual Women," and "Married Women Seeking Men" were the rooms I would frequent most.

I've always loved women. I love the way they walk, talk, smell, taste, feel, move, smile, dress, and dance, and, yes, on a general basis, they type quite well too! I always made it a point to tell the truth in chat rooms; liars have to have good memories. When I came upon someone who I thought would be interesting to converse with, we would almost inevitably trade physical stats with each other. My description was fairly standard: six foot two inches, 210 pounds, short brown hair with dark brown eyes, in good shape, with olive skin, a clean-shaven face, and, except for obvious areas, mostly hairless. Occasionally they would ask, "How 'big' are you?" and I would usually reply, "Probably not big enough to be considered porn-star material but big enough to make you squirm and squeal with delight!" I could have said anything but they always seemed to enjoy that answer. Sometimes they believed my description of myself and sometimes they didn't. I didn't care; a physical encounter wasn't what I was looking for.

Although lesbians and bisexual women are big turn-ons for me, I usually found most of my luck in the "Married Women Seeking Men" areas, where the women appeared to be the most responsive and seemingly displayed sincere interest. It wasn't often that they would volunteer a great sexual story in return, but they were usually intrigued by the true story I had to offer.

☆ ☆ ☆

I must have been his object of desire for a long time. Dave and I were the best of friends, dating back to sophomore year in high school. Together, we partied a lot, went to dozens of concerts, and often listened to the music we grew to love. We went on weekend trips together and sometimes traveled quite a distance to see new things. He encouraged me to read some of his favorite books and would offer intelligent and stimulating conversations, mostly concerning controversial issues. Dave was a slight man, which seemed to account for his not being interested in sports or women, so I didn't ask. In addition, I considered him the most cerebral person I knew and I thought that he certainly had better things to do with his time than to swing a baseball bat or attempt to compete for one of the few good-looking women in our high school.

It wasn't until later in high school that it became quite obvious that Dave was gay, and his attraction for me grew strong as time passed. One evening during one of our pot smoking/listening to music sessions in his small basement bedroom, he did openly admit that he was in fact gay. I think he had hopes that I would at least be bisexual and that I would offer a sexual experience to quench his desire.

Although this admission was no revelation, I was uncomfortable with the idea and quickly indicated that I wasn't interested in him "that way." I probably could have been a bit more subtle; he seemed crushed. Being somewhat liberal, I did accept his sexual preference and decided that it should not affect our friendship. And our friendship did thrive for years to come.

From time to time, Dave would mention that he was still infatuated with me and if I could bring myself to have sex with him just once, he could move on and pursue men who were actually gay. I understood his dilemma but was reluctant to comply. I'm certain that my negative responses only deepened his desire for me and caused some very frustrating times for him. Of course this made me feel bad, but I was not willing to give in to his persuasions—not just yet anyway.

One day Dave stated, "Don't give me an immediate reply to this; I just want you to think about it. Let's not put a time frame or a deadline on it, but if you could someday break down and have sex with me, I promise that I will never ask you again. I can then get you out of my system and I will redirect my efforts into seeking other men. This encounter will be completely on your terms, whenever and wherever you want. Just please don't answer now."

Inside I felt that this was actually a reasonable request, but it wouldn't be until a couple of years later that I would finally grant Dave's wish. And yes, Dave would stay a virgin, thinking and hoping that I would someday "set him free," allowing him to open his feelings for other men. Patience is a virtue. We remained good friends.

Some time after high school, I joined the military (without Dave's knowledge) to pursue a career and a chance to see more of the world. The economy was going south, good jobs were rare, I didn't have any money for college, and I had built up some debt that I desperately wanted to clear. Thirty days later, I said good-bye to my family, friends, and my best friend Dave. As I hopped on a bus for boot camp, Dave was obviously very upset, but what could he do?

Several states away, I breezed through basic and advanced training in eighteen weeks and was then assigned to my permanent duty station. We had written to each other several times during this period, Dave often expressing his distaste for my career decision and making a point of citing the many negative concepts the military represented. I generally accepted his ridicule and opinions and wrote off his bitterness, understanding that he missed me and wished that we lived closer.

I dated a few local ladies, met a nice woman at a dance club, fell in love, eloped, and got married all in a few short months. Some time later, I received a letter. It read, "Guess what? I'm moving in a couple of weeks and I'll only be about a half an hour drive from you! What do you think about that?" I wrote him back stating that I thought it was great and I was looking forward to seeing him again.

Dave packed up what few things he owned, moved to a city about twenty-five miles north of where I was stationed, and was gainfully employed within a week. I introduced him to my new bride, and over the next few months the three of us had some dinners and saw a concert by The Cure. My wife and Dave didn't really hit it off that well but seemed to tolerate each other for my sake. Even though my wife didn't claim to pick up on Dave's sexual preference, it was quite obvious that Dave and I were close.

Thereafter, say once or twice a week, I would drive to Dave's apartment, where we would sit around getting high, listen to music, and converse. On occasion, we would go to a nearby Italian restaurant and have a nice dinner. His feelings for me hadn't changed. After all this time, the infatuation and desire were still raging and his request was still outstanding. I had been giving some recent thought to how and when I was going to quench his thirst for me.

My wife had a business trip coming up and would be out of town for three days. I knew this about a week ahead of time but did not confer with Dave about the possibility.

After I saw my wife off, I targeted the next evening for my encounter with Dave. Although sex with another man was not foremost in my erotic thoughts, the anticipation of what was about to happen was actually quite exciting. I refrained from relieving myself sexually that evening and the next morning. I had a difficult time keeping Dave off of my mind, and the workday was going painfully slow.

It was a chilly, damp, February evening, and the night fell quickly. I grabbed a quick bite to eat, jumped in my VW, and started heading north. As I drove, I got high and smoked a couple of cigarettes, attempting to visualize just what might occur this evening. Some anxiety and a lot of excitement were building as I approached the outskirts of this large city, knowing that I would be knocking on Dave's door in just a few minutes.

Big-city parking sucks. I managed to find a spot about a block from his high-rise apartment. I quickly negotiated the many flights of stairs to his door. Hesitating for a moment, I rapped a few times on the door and heard Dave calling from inside, "Come in!" I opened the door, sauntered in, and spotted Dave across the apartment busy with something. "Hey, Scott, how are you?" I didn't answer. I immediately took out a pen and my 2" × 2" stack of yellow sticky notes and wrote, "Hi, I'm an Ellen Jamesian."[1] I tore the page off of the pad and handed it to him. "What's this?" he asked with a perplexed look on his face. I immediately wrote another: "I won't be talking this evening." Followed by, "Tonight is THE night." It didn't take him but a couple of moments to figure out what I was referring to. His confused expression promptly converted into a big smile with some noticeable blushing. Dave responded, "I'd rather get a hotel than stay here." I wrote, "Okay," and flashed him the note.

Dave's apartment was one large room with a bathroom off of one corner and a kitchenette in the opposite corner. He had a single bed without frame or headboard, a small table with two folding chairs, music equipment, and what seemed to be countless cassette tapes and albums stacked about his bare, tiled floor. His choice to go to a hotel was perfectly fine with me.

Dave grabbed his coat and gathered up a couple of items, and we were off into the brisk night. We walked at a good clip, and our silent excursion to a nearby hotel took only about ten minutes. It was a mid-size, older hotel but was kept up nicely and decorated well. Dave paid a middle-aged man at the front desk who was looking both of us over with suspicious glances. We both laughed a little and headed upstairs to our room. We moved inside and locked the door behind us. "Nice room," I jotted down and showed the note to Dave. He agreed by nodding.

It was a cozy room situated five floors above the well-lit street. A firm double bed was in the center of the room. There was a three-quarter bath directly inside the entryway.

As I was finishing my cigarette, Dave sat on the bed, looked my way, raised his eyebrows, and held his hands up and out as if to say,

1. Dave and I had both read John Irving's *The World According to Garp* (New York: Dutton, 1978), and this was a reference to a group of self-mutilated mute women protesting and representing a young raped girl by the name of Ellen James. The group called themselves "Ellen Jamesians."

"Well?" I put the cigarette out and wrote a quick note, "No kissing, no talking." Dave acknowledged the boundaries, undressed, lay back on the bed, and began stroking his dick.

While watching him lie there for a moment, the "Thin White Duke"[2] was the first thing that popped into my mind. Dave stood about five foot ten inches, had pale white skin, and weighed a thin 135 pounds. He had ice-blue eyes and short blond hair. A deep voice, a prominent Adam's apple, and a patch of blond chest hair kept his appearance on the masculine side. As I watched him play with his package while looking at me, I immediately took note of his very large penis head. I'd only seen one that large in porno and began to wonder what kind of discomfort this might cause. Having gone this far, there was no way to smoothly back out of the situation. I dismissed the negative thought, stripped off my clothes, and laid them neatly over a chair.

I turned around and walked over to the bed, where Dave was now sitting upright. I stood in front of him half-erect and positioned myself directly in line with his face. With a smile, he glanced up with glassy eyes, grabbed my prick with one hand, stroked it two or three times, and started going down on me. I hardened quickly; Dave worked up and down my length, popping my dick out of his mouth a couple of times only to move down to suck and lick my balls. Drawing one nut into his mouth, tonguing it back and forth and alternating with the other, he soon had me so hard I thought I was going to explode right then and there. I placed my hands on his shoulders to push him back slightly, encouraging him to stop for righ now.

I motioned to him to get up in the bed and he complied, placing his head near the pillows. With my straining erection, I got into the bed with my head toward the footboard, both of us now lying on our right sides facing each other. Dave eagerly went to work again, wrapping his hot, wet lips around my cock and hammering his head like a

2. David Bowie called himself "The Thin White Duke" on the opening track of his 1976 album *Station to Station*.

piston. Unlike the hetero blow jobs I was accustomed to, the strength of his mouth felt tremendous!

I began to lick and kiss his blood-engorged dick and large balls as he continued to hungrily suck on mine. I opened wide and placed his big bulb inside of my mouth, twirling my tongue around the rim, and began sliding his throbbing unit to the back of my throat. Although it felt somewhat suffocating and awkward, the feeling of having another man's penis in my mouth became very exciting. I could feel the veins of my manhood strain so hard that they began to ache with pleasure. The sensation arising from this event was no different from what I would think sucking on one's own cock would feel like, without the backache. What a thrill!

I resumed stroking his shaft with my mouth, his bulbous head making it difficult not to catch him with my teeth. On occasion, I would pull him out of my mouth, catch some air, suck on his balls, and then draw his rod back into my mouth. Dave wet his fingers with his saliva and worked his middle finger into my asshole. After a few strokes, his index finger joined in, and he began sliding them in and out of my ass, creating new sensations toward a mounting climax. I responded by reciprocating, sometimes mimicking the same rhythm.

After a minute or two of this added turn-on, I just couldn't hold back any longer. With thirty-six hours of anticipation built up, my once-swinging balls drew up tight to my body and the pleasure spasms began, wave after wave. Trying not to lose all muscle control, I concentrated on holding my pelvis still while the eruption continued. Dave's mouth quickly filled with ejaculate and he swallowed; his mouth filled again and again he swallowed. I didn't think my orgasm was going to stop. Finally, the awesome feelings subsided and I rolled to my back, exhausted. Dave kept sucking and jacking me off softly, siphoning every last joy drop I had to offer. This "rookie" just gave me the best blow job of my life! I thought to myself, *He'll certainly please a lot of men. . . .*

After a short rest, still on the bed, I turned my attention back to Dave, slid his cock back into my mouth, and went to work. Thankful for my great head job, I went back to sucking him off the best that

I could, kneading his balls with the palm of my hand while thrusting two fingers in and out of his butthole. I think he was about to come once or twice, but I had to let up and rest for a moment from time to time. After several minutes, my mouth grew weary and I could no longer hold the "O" needed to avoid using any teeth. My lips were numb, my jaw was sore, and Dave—he was still very excited.

During the last pause, I started jacking him off using slow and fast strokes, squeezing a little and then letting up, focusing a little extra pressure on the underside and to the top of his shaft. His positive reaction to this prompted me to continue stroking him. I imagined how I masturbated and I tried to provide the same feeling for him. His moans of approval and the tightening of his balls told me I was doing it right. After a few short minutes of this, Dave bucked his pelvis a couple of times, groaned deeply from within and began to come. Warm, thick streams of jism started flying everywhere—all over his shaking body, onto the floor, onto the pillows, onto the bedspread, and his last couple of shots dripped over my hand. I went on to stroke him gently until the last of his juice seeped out of his large knob. He seemed quite satisfied and pleased with the outcome of this episode.

We rolled out of bed and climbed into the shower together. We quietly and thoroughly soaped and scrubbed ourselves up and down, rinsed, dried, and headed back into the room. Lighting another cigarette and still naked, we silently sat back on the bed. Just as I had finished smoking, Dave reached into his coat, pulled out a small white bottle of lubricant, and placed it on the bed. I obviously knew what that was for. Without hesitation, Dave turned my way, knelt on the floor, positioned his head between my legs, and began licking and sucking my package into another large hard-on. Satisfied that it was as big and hard as it was going to get, Dave grabbed the slippery sauce and began to apply it all over my cock. He then easily slid two fingers up into my ass, and I got even harder. After withdrawing his fingers, he picked up the lube and began to put generous amounts on and around his awaiting asshole. I knew what was going to happen next, and my excitement grew. He centered himself on the bed on all fours and motioned to me that he was ready. I climbed up on the bed and squared myself behind him.

Dave seemed a bit anxious and nervous. His small, firm, white ass was poised up in the air, willing to take whatever I had to offer. To assure accommodation, I inserted two and then three fingers into his hot, slick hole and worked them in and out until I felt his sphincter relax somewhat. After this action, I was super excited and ready to get off without any penetration! Nevertheless, I got up on my knees and pushed the head of my manhood just inside his glistening, puckered opening. I then inched about one half of my rod up his ass and checked with him to make sure he was okay. He was accepting to this point, without much apparent discomfort, so I partially withdrew and then drove the entire length of my dick all the way up his ass. He let out a low grunt and didn't indicate that we had a problem. His gripping asshole felt like a wet, silky vise as I established a pace to provide him with a good butt-fucking. I would have loved to screw his sweet, virgin ass for an hour, but unfortunately my climax was just around the bend. A cock-ring would have been perfect just then! I probably didn't even get in twenty strokes. My balls began to ache and tighten, my dick stiffened to its capacity, and my lower abdomen began to contract with warm waves. I thought, *Too bad this is going so quick,* as I firmly latched onto his hips and vigorously pumped his ass full of come with a loud series of moans and groans from both of us. Although this orgasm was not as long as the first, it was every bit as strong, if not stronger. Reluctantly, because I was spent, I withdrew my dwindling hard-on and we collapsed together on the bed.

Several minutes passed, and I caught my breath, recovered some energy, and sat up. Noticing that Dave was partially aroused, I suppose from the ass-pounding he had just received, I reached over and fondled him again. I was again fixated on his large dick head and was contemplating what would happen next. Surmising that it was now my turn to be on the receiving end of anal sex, I believe Dave sensed my growing anxiety. Not wanting to subject me to possible pain, Dave decided to take a different route.

With his prick now at full attention, he lay back on the bed, folded his hands behind his neck, and pasted a grin on his face. I began to jack him off as I had before, and he nodded his head with approval. I really wanted to make this nice for him, so I again focused on how I pleasure myself and tried to duplicate the motions. Changing speed and grip strength, I varied the sensations to observe his best reaction. His facial expressions and primal sounds acknowledged that I had again found the right combination. The concentration of keeping this stimulation steady for a few minutes generated the approach of another strong climax for Dave. His breathing grew heavy. I didn't miss a stroke. He gyrated his hips a little. I stayed right with him. He paused for a moment and let out a loud groan as copious amounts of hot semen began to spurt all about. The waves of pleasure and thin, shooting ribbons of white come soon subsided and I lay down next to him on the bed. We both broke a sweat on that one!

After a few minutes of lying there, we gathered our senses and climbed out of bed. We dressed and sat at the table overlooking the lit-up city. Dave appeared satiated. He watched me smoke a last cigarette and indicated that we should leave. I agreed.

We exited the room and the hotel and walked together into the night. On the way home I had written another note: "Are you okay?" He responded by nodding and offering an ear-to-ear smile. I wrote, "Would you like to keep all of the notes?" He wrinkled up his nose and shook his head back and forth. I gathered the notes from my pocket, balled them up, and tossed them into a nearby trash can.

We made our way back to his apartment building and slowly climbed the stairs to his room. He motioned for me to come in and I just stood there in the doorway. Realizing that I wasn't coming in, Dave turned around, wrapped both of his arms around me, and said, "Thank you, Scott." Hugging him back I said, "Good night." We let go of each other, and I was gone.

Two decades later, Dave and I are still great friends. Dave did move on and was able to redirect his efforts and emotions to more physically fruitful relationships. Dave moved about the country—

and the world—pulling up his roots every three to five years. There were times when we lost contact for a year or so, but we would catch back up to each other and bring our lives current, sometimes talking for hours.

With the passage of time, on reflection, that night was very positive for both of us, though I didn't realize it at the time. If you ever have one person in your life that you can call a true friend, consider yourself rich. I'm rich.

☆8☆ And the Straight Shall Be Crooked

Steve Kokker

Thursday was cheap night at the Makarenko *banya*. Entrance to these public baths was just six rubles (about eighteen cents), instead of the usual twenty rubles. Thursday nights usually attracted pensioners and invalids, stooping, elderly men with great, long scars, welts, and other signs of imperfect medical tampering across their bodies, limping old souls with swollen bellies or elephantitis in the testes. They'd hobble from the changing room into the shower and washing area, then into the hot steam room, clutching bands of birch branches in one hand, steadying themselves on paint-chipped walls with the other.

Yet in this motley Thursday night mix were always two or three—never more, never less—devastatingly fine young men. Students and military cadets, poor or simply frugal.

I always enjoyed the public baths on these discount days, partially to read the lives of the old men through their scarred bodies; many were war veterans (a medal or two was sometimes pinned onto the tattered dark jackets left dangling on the changing room coat hooks). Yet I'm no pensioner fetishist.

My attention was most fervently taken up by the few attractive young men who strode among those sublimely grotesque figures. Perhaps they appeared all the more appealing because of the striking contrast they offered to the withered masses, but their youth, virility, and beauty seemed to radiate in defiance of the sad visions of aging flesh which surrounded them. Thursday nights in St. Petersburg were always memorable for me.

I remember first spotting the regulation blue-striped undershirt hanging up in the changing room, a poorly lit but expansive space whose high ceilings dripped of condensation. Four rows of about fifteen oversized, upright wooden chairs pushed up against one another took the place of lockers. Wide enough only to sit on, these chairs doubled as coat racks; above people's heads their often dirty clothes ignominiously spilled down from small metal hooks. The sight of military academy uniforms hanging from those hooks always excited me and made me look out for their naked owners in the showers or steam bath. No one, except for the rare Muslim visitor, ever wore anything while walking around.

This night, just as I noticed the one striped undershirt in the place, a young man of nineteen or twenty walked up to it, yanked it off, and returned to the larger, adjacent room where people sat on stone benches and laboriously washed themselves. He was fetchingly attractive, if somewhat awkwardly so.

Tousled black hair topped an angular, friendly face whose high cheekbones and rosy cheeks were its prominent features. He was so slim he'd be considered skinny by American standards, but his chest, arms, and legs were toned and strong. He had a slight duck walk. His penis was lovely—longish, slightly bent to the right, backed by a mat of fine black hair that would thankfully never fall prey to the tedious, fey practice of clipping or shaving. Most notable of all were his incredibly long testicles which hung and swayed low.

After a few minutes of sitting alone, convincing myself to approach this boy, I pushed open the creaky wooden door separating the changing room from the washing area and made my way to where I saw him from behind stooping over the stone bench, arms moving back and forth rigorously, bits of soap flying. Though my focus was at first on his hard, round buttocks and the dangling sac falling in between them, I saw that he was washing his undershirt in a soapy basin. The *banyas* don't allow people to bring in their dirty clothes to be washed, but they make an exception for military cadets.

Nervous, I had repeated to myself for the last five minutes what I'd say to him, and, heart thumping, I walked up to him and asked in broken Russian, "Excuse me, but are you a military cadet?" He flipped his head up toward me, never stopping his washing, and shook a loose clump of hair that had fallen over his eyes. He was smiling broadly, his eyes wide open and enthusiastic, rosy cheeks dancing. *I'm sure my eyes glistened unashamedly.*

"Da!"

"I was just wondering where I might be able to buy one of those striped undershirts—I've been looking everywhere!"

With that he stood up straight and, still smiling with puppylike friendliness, cocked his head slightly and asked, "Where are you from?"

"Canada."

"Canada! A Canadian at the *banya?* I don't believe it. What are you doing here?"

I chose to take that as why was I in Russia instead of at the *banya* and told him I was teaching English and French, learning Russian, trying to figure out the country and its people.

He introduced himself as Ivan, and we shook hands, both of us stark naked, dripping with sweat and condensation. We began a lively exchange. The old men nearby stared at us with idle curiosity. Ivan was from a small village of about two thousand people in southern Russia. His family had one cow, he told me proudly, and several chickens. He had come to St. Petersburg to become a naval officer, the first member of his family to receive higher education.

After rinsing out his soapy, sodden undershirt, he looked at me almost mischievously and asked, "Want to help me?"

"Yeah!" I answered immediately. "Do what?"

He handed me one arm of the shirt, but I looked at him blankly. I had helped my mother fold sheets like this but couldn't figure out why I needed to help him fold his shirt. He angled his body slightly sideways and stuck one foot out toward me at a right angle to my body. He winsomely nodded for me to do the same. I pressed my foot against his, we each grabbed onto one arm of the shirt and started twisting and pulling it away from each other. It looked as if we wanted to rip it to shreds, but soon the water was pouring out from the material. We were human wringers.

"Didn't you ever do this before?" he asked, spotting my obvious lack of expertise. I shook my head. "This is the navy way to dry clothes!" he announced, twisting with all his strength.

In my defense, I was flustered partly because I was standing with my foot pressed against a delectable, naked, dripping cadet, helping him wring out his military undershirt in a public *banya.* I pretended to see a cinematic long shot of the both of us and thought to myself with schoolgirl glee, *I don't believe I'm doing this!*

I doubt he could have quite appreciated my frazzled state.

We both seemed very enthusiastic about having met each other. After drying off and dressing up for the cold, March drizzle that awaited us on the streets, he took down my phone number, promising to call. He didn't want me to call him at the academy—a call from a foreigner would lead to questions he could do without.

Ivan called as promised within a few days, and he dropped by my apartment for a visit, something he ended up doing regularly over the next few months. We got along so well, we were so excited and happy every time we met, it almost threw me for a loop.

Ivan turned out to be so sweet, so naive about life, so good-natured and trusting ("A mere country boy!" huffed one of my more jaded Russian friends about him), I couldn't bring myself to broach the subject of sex at first. He was so genuinely physical, so affectionate, even without being plied with vodka, that I hardly even felt a great desire to push things further. Fascinated with every detail about the workings of my laptop, for example, he'd sit close to me on an adjacent chair, his leg pressed up against mine, almost entwining with mine, and he'd think nothing of draping a lazy arm around my shoulder, smiling at me inches away from my face. We pretended to be engrossed in key clicks and car race games but were really into this heavy platonic intimacy. We'd hug when we greeted and parted, when a good song came on the radio, or when we just looked at each other and felt like it.

This buddy romance would have gone on indefinitely if I hadn't somehow (awkwardly, as I recall) told him that I was attracted to men. Russian men, I already knew from experience, would have little problem sleeping and having sex with you but only if you were straight, like them. But frame it as something *goluboi* (gay; literally, "blue"), let them peer into that abyss, and the date's off. Still, Ivan had proved himself to be so genuine, I couldn't bring myself to pretend or be manipulative for the sake of a romp in the sack.

He was quite shocked at the revelation, asked a dozen questions, and for a few days the hugs and near cuddling stopped. Finally, he stated, "Steve, you're my great friend, but this is incomprehensible to me. Please don't feel badly, but there's no way I can do something like that! I only have sex with girls!" I assured him that was fine by me, as long as we remained friends.

Our relationship deepened over the next few months. The revelation of my sexuality opened up the general topic of sex, which once opened, overtook all other conversational topics. He told me of the girls he'd bedded since moving from his village to St. Petersburg and asked me what men do together.

One September evening we had one of the most intense talks of my life. In the small kitchen of my rented Marata Street flat, which overlooked a courtyard and into Dostoyevsky's last apartment, where he had died, Ivan's voice started to crack. He always slipped into falsetto squeaks when he got excited or nervous.

"Steve!" he said, furrowing his brow. "I lied to you!" His fist came down on his knee. "I never had sex with a girl in my life! I'm a virgin!"

In the ensuing hours, I had a raw look at Ivan's many complexes (in the Western sense of the word; these would simply be called personality traits in any other culture). I had thus far not encountered a Russian guy with physical "hang-ups" of the kind that can emotionally paralyze men back home. In Russia, if you were a bit overweight, thin, unmuscular, pale, hairy-chested (or, rather, undepilated), or born with a less than adequately sized penis, well, that's just the way it was. You get on with life and concentrate on more important things.

"But Ivan, why didn't you tell me before?"

"I didn't want you to think I was a loser. I'm ashamed of it!"

"Man, I wouldn't have. Are you just too shy to have sex or . . . ?"

"I don't know. I tried, but it just wouldn't work!" He poured himself one vodka after another and started downing them.

"No erection?"

He just shook his head. "I wanted to. I was just too scared."

"Of what?" I placed my hand on his shoulder as he looked at the floor, shaking his head, distraught at the memory. It took a while for him to blurt out the reason, but when he did, he screamed it.

"I have a crooked penis!"

I sat, puzzled for a moment. I had seen his penis many times at our *banya* sessions. It had a very slight rightward bend, nothing unusual. Thick and nice-looking too. I told him so.

"No!" Now his eyes brimmed with tears. "It's bent! Steve, it's so horrible!" With that, I leaned forward and hugged him close. "I've never told anyone this," he cried. I let him sob onto my shoulder as I stroked his head, myself awash with emotions ranging from compassion to surprise at this sudden dramatic disclosure.

It turned out that he had long harbored a fear that his penis would not be able to penetrate a woman properly and, to avoid a disastrously embarrassing incident, he avoided all sexual situations.

I assured him that his penis was hardly bent at all, that nearly half of all men have some degree of curvature in their penises, that I'd seen other ones, perfectly functional, much more crooked than his, and that vaginas are large and forgiving enough to accept pretty much whatever's given them.

While I knew he had no reason to worry so, I could hardly fault him for being foolish—I had had my own period of struggling with a similar complex. "Ivan," I ventured, "I know how you feel, believe me. When I was your age I thought that my cock was too small, and to avoid embarrassment I avoided sexual situations literally for years. Now I see how silly it was, but I hope you won't deny yourself pleasure as I did for something that's mostly in your mind."

"You have a normal cock," he said.

"It's not so big."

"But it's straight!"

As the discussion seemed always to revert back to the degree and extent of his bend, I suggested he take his penis out to face facts, as it were. He was shy to do this, but I could tell he also wanted to. After dismissing my suggestion, he got up to piss and, from the toilet, called out, "It looks so crooked!" which was my cue to show up for an examination. He'd left the door open, so I just stepped in with him as he stood there, genitals exposed outside his dark blue uniform trousers. I took his penis in my hand for the first time and told him that his bend was insignificant, that he had a great prick and especially beautiful balls.

He zipped up and we returned to the kitchen, where we spoke more calmly about his general nervousness with girls. He said he didn't feel like a real man being a virgin, and that he'd resigned himself to remaining that way his entire life.

"That's overly dramatic," I offered, "even for a Russian. Everything will be fine." The outburst was over and his cock had been examined; some corner had been turned.

Over the next few weeks the topic came up again and again; he seemed to like hearing me repeat the same words of encouragement. I also half-jokingly suggested we fool around together as a way to initiate him into the world of sex. He'd smile sweetly, shake his head, and say, "No thanks, Steve."

Soon after, I left the country for about six months. Before we parted, he presented me with a few photos as mementos: him milking his one dear cow back home; him shirtless on a far north nuclear submarine military base; him shirtless in a park in Pushkin, outside St. Petersburg. On the back of each he had written expressive sentiments with many exclamation marks, like, "Thank you for the understanding!"

The following year I was in and out of St. Petersburg and would see Ivan every few months. This time, we became physically closer than ever before. He remembered that I'd once given him an especially attentive massage and asked for a repeat. We then got into the habit of giving each other protracted massages lasting an hour or more, or until he had to run out, flag down a car, and get back to his academy before his curfew.

He'd lay in his regulation boxers and nearly purr under my ministrations. He'd ask me questions about what I thought of different parts of his body, negating my compliments with his own self-deprecating comments. He'd giggle like a child whenever I'd take his long, perennially loose ball sac into my hands and tell him how beautiful it was ("They're only balls!" he'd exclaim, laughing, twisting his body away). He sometimes squirmed shyly but clearly loved the attention. I'd occasionally cup my hand over his cock and gently keep it there the few seconds he'd let go by before pushing my hand aside. I was aware that these sessions were the only moments of physical intimacy in his life.

He'd also tell me about his aborted attempts to get close to girls he'd meet at the academy dances. The loosely dressed, heavily made-up girls who hung out outside military academies, I always thought, were much bigger sluts than even I. I and my fellow military admirers would always smugly deride them for their lack of subtlety, for their inability to provide the cadets with the company they loved and respected most: male. Only we, we often gloated, could offer them the comradeship the cadets seemed to thrive on *plus* uncomplicated sex. Of course, we were also jealous at the ease with which the girls could get into the cadets' pants—pass by dark corners near any academy, peer into the bushes in nearby courtyards or into the darkened, crumbling staircases of next-door apartment buildings, and you'd be sure to spy a young couple screwing.

Yet it seemed Ivan couldn't even land these easy targets. He'd get so nervous he'd drink himself into a useless state of oblivion, or he'd get into a potentially intimate situation, then get so anxious that the girl would discover his anomaly, he would lose all ability to get hard and back out.

I left Russia again, and it was another six months that I didn't see Ivan. In the meantime I called him at his small village home a few times from Canada, and we'd exchange postcards.

Once back in St. Petersburg, I got in touch with him again. It was our third year of knowing each other.

This time when he showed up at my door, I could sense something new and more assured about him. He'd let his hair grow longer, and it fell in front of his right eye with a casual, self-assured sexiness he'd not let himself exhibit before. He hugged me tight when we greeted, lifting me up off the floor, then set me down and looked at me long in the eyes, his big smile at first inscrutable.

I immediately asked him if he'd had sex. It felt like he'd had. His face clouded up and I regretted my question. No. It hadn't happened.

"Never mind," I said. "How about a massage? Like old times." He smiled and was walking off to the bedroom before I'd even finished the invitation. While we chattered about what had happened recently in each other's lives, he peeled off his shirt and lay down on his stomach expectantly. I climbed atop him and resumed the familiar motions of my hands. I told him he felt more muscular than before. "I swim every day!" he announced proudly.

Later, he sat up against a pillow on the bed and looked at me expectantly, smiling. Every fiber of my well-developed but often ignored intuition told me he wanted sex with me, but it took a little testing for me to be certain enough to proceed further. Not that there could be any offense between us after all we'd been through together. I cupped his genitals through his boxers with my hand and asked how it could be that such great things had still not been put to use. He giggled in response and ever so lightly moved his hips upward.

I kept my hand firmly over his now stirring penis and balls. I started a massaging motion which produced a rapid erection and a louder giggle from Ivan. "It seems ready for action!" I said, and slowly manipulated his penis out of the fly of his boxers.

He'd shown me his erection before, but in a rather medical context, as we tried to ascertain the degree of his bendedness. Yet this time there was a sexual energy in the air. His hands, placed at his side, were not halfheartedly pushing mine away, and his dick was pulsating against my palm in tremulous anticipation. I continued rubbing it and watched him twitch with pleasure.

I then bent my head down and took a tentative lick along his frenulum. A little giggle again, but this time an absentminded one. It was exactly what he wanted. I bent further and took his cock in my mouth, slowly at first, then whole. I felt his whole body twitch as I closed my lips on his shaft. I was suddenly aware that no one else had ever done this to him before.

I continued giving him a blow job, but I tried to keep the pace slow and irregular, as I felt he was ready to come immediately. I closed my eyes and tried to savor every moment, every sensation. I felt as much a sexual thrill as an emotional one, knowing what trust this act implied for him. I buried my nose into his fine, hairy bush and kept it there, increasing pressure along his shaft and continuing to suck slowly.

Then I unwittingly made a wrong move. I drew my head back and pulled down his boxers. I wanted to get my lips on his long sac as well. But as soon as his boxers were bunched up on his upper thigh, he lost his erection, even as I continued sucking. I pretended not to notice and just went on. But once it had started retreating, there was no turning back. I could feel his body tense up. I knew from personal experience that he undoubtedly was going to let self-consciousness snowball into fear and embarrassment and that nothing could reverse the process.

Sure enough, he wiggled out from under my head, apologized, and pulled his boxers up. I asked what had happened, but knew that even such a minor gesture as removing his underwear was enough to switch on his enormous self-consciousness and ruin his concentration. He said that it had felt good, he liked it, but he just couldn't go on.

He then looked at me and asked hesitantly, "How was I?"

"Great! Um, but what do you mean?"

"How did I feel?"

"Oh that," I said, realizing he wanted to know if his penis, bent as it was, felt any different to me. "Ivan, no, it felt wonderful. I couldn't notice anything different, it was great. Delicious." I leaned over to kiss his cheek. "But next time we'll take it slower. Okay?"

"Yes." He nodded and attempted a smile, but his face was clouded over.

The next time came about three days later. He came over in a good mood as usual and walked to the bedroom as soon as he had removed his naval cap and overcoat. He half sat, half lay on the bed, and I reclined next to him. We chatted about the last few days and I placed my arm across his stomach. His body language focused on his crotch. I knew he wanted a blow job.

I moved my hand down over his crotch. He was already hard. I unzipped him, and this time he helped me pull his blue uniform pants and boxers off, down to his knees. I descended upon his cock hungrily and started sucking. He let out a short breath. This time his control seemed better so I allowed myself to quicken the pace and increase the pressure. I also paused long enough to push my face between his thighs and work his lovely testicles, hanging long and loose between his legs and now folding themselves over my cheek. I looked up at him and saw his head arched upward, eyes closed, lips clenched. I licked around his perineum and felt his thighs contract on either side of my face.

I continued sucking him for another few minutes until he lifted a hand to touch my face but stopped halfway. "I'm coming," he breathed out. Even then he thought to be considerate. I increased the pace until I felt a hot burst hit the back of my throat, followed quickly by another. He arched his midriff upward and let out a long moan, letting go of another few spurts of ejaculate.

When the waves of his orgasm had died down, I looked up at him to see him with his eyes still closed, but wearing a wide smile. "Wow," he said. "That felt so great."

He bounced off the bed, zipped himself up, and went to pour himself a Pepsi. I sat on the edge of the bed and smiled as I heard him humming in the kitchen. He walked back into the bedroom and happily announced, "I guess this means I'm a man now!"

As that evening came only days before I was to leave St. Petersburg once again for a protracted period, he managed to come over a few more times for repeat performances. At twenty-two years old, he'd discovered his third leg and was at least momentarily insatiable. I had no problem attending to his newly discovered love of getting blow jobs.

The last evening we met, after he'd put on his navy overcoat for the last time, he hugged me tight, lifting me off the ground. "Thank you so much!"

The following spring, Ivan graduated from his naval academy and after a brief holiday back home in his village was shipped off to a far east naval base outside Vladivostok, eight time zones away. He still keeps in touch occasionally via brief e-mails when he gets access to a terminal on base, and I sometimes call his mom to hear whatever latest news she has. I've never been able to find out if he ever did sleep with a girl, but he'll be getting vacation time in a few months and we already have plans to meet up in St. Petersburg.

☆9☆

Motorcycle Boy

Pete

He really did look like a misfit. His ash-blond hair was cropped short and Marinelike, fresh cut and smelling of Barbicide. If it were longer he would have looked ridiculously like a bottle brush or a pin cushion. But it was just right, the way I like it. He had a smile that made his lips curl in a funny and wicked sort of way. His eyes were liquid blue and pleading.

I liked him the moment I saw him. He wasn't tall or particularly pretty. He really didn't have a package. But he was a sailor and he looked and smelled like it. And, well, all he wanted to do was buy me a beer.

We played eye contact tag. He was talking to a much older man, white haired and wearing a black leather jacket. Most definitely gay, most definitely annoyed with my presence. Motorcycle Boy, on the other hand, didn't show any stereotypical gay traits. In fact, he was very ungay-looking, all the way down to his Machinist Mate Second Class fingernails, his dirty and ripped Levi's, and his sailor swagger.

He came up next to me, ordered a Bud Light, and said hi to me with a big silly grin that made him look more stupid than he really was. We chatted about computers and stuff for awhile. I was still unable to check him as interested or just an overly friendly lonely guy. Throughout the conversation he continually lifted his shirt and readjusted his red-tag 501's, which were at least three sizes too big. I know he caught me trying to see what sort of underwear he wore. But he didn't have any on and so what he saw me catching a glimpse of was his pubic hair.

When he finished his beer he said, "Sorry, I have to go." He put on a black motorcycle jacket, a black helmet, and one of those orange hunter vests. I stuttered that I too must go and that I lived only a short distance away and usually walked home. He gave me that almost Gomer Pyle-ish dopey smile and said that he could drop me off.

Yeah, right. Uh-huh, I thought. I knew where this was going. It was going to my bedroom, and I didn't mind.

Climbing on the back of his dented Honda 650cc I squeezed my crotch tight against his backside. I didn't put my hands on him, opting instead to brace my arms behind me on the back of the seat handle. He didn't seem to mind; in fact, he leaned his body back against me, which only heightened the sexual tension. And then we were off.

In less than a minute we were in front of my house and I was mumbling an invitation to come in and have a beer for the road.

"No," he said. "I've had enough. Maybe some other time."

He slipped down the visor on his helmet, revved his bike, and was off, just like that, with me standing there thinking how fucking funny it was that I had misread his cues.

☆☆☆

I am very careful about the sailors I approach. Usually I prefer to let them approach me. It's safer that way.

The next time I saw Motorcycle Boy he virtually ignored me, spending the evening talking to a woman and then that same older man with the black leather jacket. *Fine,* I thought, *so he really is just one of those nice lonely guys that likes to chat with everyone.* And so it came as a surprise when the next evening he stopped by my house unannounced on his way to the bar and, with a very serious expression, said he had a question to ask me.

"Can I sleep here tonight? I want to have a good time, but I don't want to go back on base drunk."

I blinked. "Um, sure you can. I got a big couch and two spare rooms."

"You know, you are pretty cool." He grabbed my shoulder and squeezed it pretty hard. And he gave me this look that I can't describe, but for the first time it made me see that there was something off balance with him.

At the bar there was a party for his ship, so a lot of his shipmates were there. He ordered *two* pitchers of Bud Light. He drank and he drank. Soon he was at the stage where he was grabbing women and pulling them on the dance floor, gyrating and caterwauling all over the place. He was making a spectacle of himself. Once again I reflected that he must be straight as he sat chatting up one of the local "WESTPAC widows" [Navy wives whose husbands are out to sea on six-month Western Pacific cruises].

Whenever we made eye contact he seemed to give me a knowing glance. As the night wore on, however, he was looking more and more at the floor. The club owner, a friend of mine, suggested that Motorcycle Boy needed to go home as he was cut off from any more beer and was looking like he was ready to crash onto the dance floor.

He didn't offer much resistance as I dragged him out into the cool night air. We walked the short distance to my house in the ghetto neighborhood adjacent to the base. He was sobering up now. He seemed to walk a little straighter. Did I say straighter? I mean more erect—er, I'm not sure what I mean, but I was beginning to feel my pulse quicken as we went in the front door and sat down on my leather couch. We sat there and he tried to explain some odd theory of his pertaining to the primitive spiritual world existing inside computers. I was having a hard time keeping my eyes open and was just about ready to leave him on the couch when he blurted out, "Sometimes me and my shipmates get real tense working on the ship. So we take turns giving each other back rubs. You know, to relax."

"Oh yeah? Well, my last roommate was a masseuse and she taught me some massage techniques," I mumbled.

"If you want we can go up to your room and try to give each other a massage to, you know, just relax after a hard night drinking."

"Sure, if you really want to—it's fine with me." I led him upstairs to my room.

I started by taking my shirt off and looking at him. He said he wanted to do my back first, so I lay face down on the bed and waited for his icy hands to touch me. They weren't icy though. They were really warm. His hands felt gritty from the calluses that covered his palms, but his touch also had a softness to it. He rubbed my shoulders and his technique felt pretty professional as he worked his way down to my lower back and waistline. He told me if I loosened my pants then he could really work my lower back. I wasted no time in loosening them and sliding them down to my knees. My loose boxers also were lowered to about half mast and my white ass must have really contrasted with his red and chapped hands.

He stalled. I took my cue. "Hey, you know what?" I said. "It's my turn to do you." As I stood up I removed my pants the rest of the way and stood there, my boxers tent poling like a Ringling Bros. and Barnum & Bailey Circus big top. I didn't try to hide it and just watched as he removed his pants. Here was one little catch in our mutual striptease, though, as he didn't have any underwear on. He lay face down quickly and I just barely glimpsed his tool, which seemed pretty average. I straddled him just below his buttocks and began to work his shoulders and neck. Leaning forward in this position forced my hard dick to be sheathed like a knife in the scabbard of his tight white ass. I still had my boxers on, but I was beginning to feel the juices stir, and they had a bit of a wet spot on the front of them.

"Oh, man. You're good," he moaned.

I told him that I like to do a full-body massage and instructed him to roll over. He did and his hard cock popped up all red and swollen. It was about five inches long but the head was so huge it looked like it should have been on a dick twice the size. It made me think of a magic mushroom.

He smiled at me and lay there very still as I straddled his dick and held it tightly in the space between my ass and my balls. I worked his hairless chest and abdomen, slowly backing up until I was leaning down and taking his cock into my mouth, all of it in one big swallow. Some guys like big dicks, but I prefer average-sized or even small ones because they are more fun to suck. There is more latitude on what sort of technique can be applied. Well, he quietly moaned and lay there, and when I felt him start to build up, I took my mouth off and he let fly with a wad that shot a good two feet in the air, landing on his face.

He looked relieved and happy but bewildered about what to do next. I rolled over beside him and put my arms behind my head. He pulled down my boxers and said to me, "I don't like to suck them."

I told him to do what he liked to do, and he gave me an okay hand job that for some reason made me fantasize about farmers with calloused hands. We curled up naked in bed and fell asleep, I dreaming of nothing and he of the motherboard used in the design of some strangely human computer, I'm sure.

Things with Motorcycle Boy were never very certain. He didn't call when he said he would; he didn't come by when he promised to. I didn't even mind. He was really nothing more than a fuck to me at that point, albeit a strange one. It got entirely more strange the second time that he came over to my house after his first-aid class.

When he came in the front door he kissed me hard and quick and asked me if I wanted to help him with some of the homework that he had from his class. I hesitantly agreed; I just wanted to know exactly what the homework was. He went back out to his bike and returned with a large gym bag that was full of stuff.

"What's in the bag?"

"Well, you know I'm taking this first-aid class and tonight we were practicing immobilizing people with casts. And I wanted to practice on you and if you want maybe you can practice on me." It was sort of naively sweet the way he talked, as if I were not aware of some ulterior motive for doing this. So I said sure and because this was supposed to be a serious exercise we subconsciously decided to use the spare bedroom for this practice session. Like before with the massage I was once again chosen to go first. In short order my pants were off and he applied a brace to my leg. When the back of his hand brushed against my crotch he could not have missed my obvious arousal.

When Motorcycle Boy was finished applying the brace he was very excited about it and very eager for my approval and praise for this contraption he had attached to my leg.

"Well, it's, er, interesting. Uh, so you guys have to all go home and practice on people?"

"No, but I just thought you might like to try this and maybe fool around a bit. You know, it's kind of exciting, don't you think?"

"It's different. Why don't I put it on you and see how you like it?"

His eyes glowed brightly and he removed the brace with a speed and dexterity that would have made his instructor proud! He took off his pants and this time he did have underwear on. He stood there in his tighty-whiteys.

I put the brace on him under his instruction. He had a neck brace in his bag that he asked me to put on him too. I complied. I was then instructed to wrap his braced arm with Ace bandage and put it in a sling. I did so. But I was losing any erection as this was turning into more of an exercise in achieving some merit badge than foreplay.

He leaned back on the bed and his dick was at full attention. *Hmmm,* I thought to myself, *Motorcycle Boy has a fetish.*

I climbed on top of him and pressed my body close against his. I pulled his arms above his head and held them tightly and kissed him on the mouth, hard. He squirmed and thrust his hips to grind with mine. He spread his legs for me and our crotches fit together like puzzle pieces found under the couch that surprisingly match. My boxers slid down easily, but I pulled and ended up tearing his underwear off. I was quite hot now and was in a sweat, which only made our sliding against each other more arousing.

I cradled his head in my hands and looked deep into his eyes. He looked at me and in the softest and most pleading voice asked, "Suck the air out of me . . . please."

"Do what? Suck the air out of you? What do you mean?"

"You know, instead of doing mouth-to-mouth and breathing out for me, inhale and suck the air out of me."

"Umm, why? That sounds kind of dangerous."

"I know, but please, I'll let you do anything if you do this."

So I tried. The first time I did it I lost my breath as he squirmed and kicked against me.

"I'm sorry—did I hurt you?"

"No. Don't stop though. I want you to hold me down hard and not let me up."

"I don't know. This is a little spooky to me. What if you pass out or die or something?"

"No, don't worry, it's okay. I've done this before and it's not dangerous. *Please* just hold me down and suck the air out of me. Just don't stop!"

His breath filled my lungs and I exhaled it through my nose. I sucked again and the smell of his breath filled my sinuses, mingled with the smell of sweat and sex. I pushed his hands down above his head and straddled his hips and spread his legs further. My cock slipped toward his ass as he positioned himself to let me inside of him. I thrust my dick toward his hole and was able to get the tip of my head into his ass. I sucked harder and harder on his mouth, putting my hands over his nose to keep him from gasping for any air. I watched his eyes for any sign of danger, but they just glazed over as I pushed myself further into him and he pushed harder toward me.

I gasped and let off, allowing him to catch a quick breath before I once again locked an air seal on him, sucking the air out of Motorcycle Boy. I slowly drove him toward the head of the bed. I was feeling very powerful as I began to master the technique for air sucking. On the next breath he said, "There is some duct tape in my bag. Tape my hands to the headboard so you can hold me down better."

"Uh, are you sure? This is, umm, pretty weird already."

"Yeah. Just do it. You are so good and you're fucking me the way I like to be fucked."

I got the duct tape and taped him up. He then told me to put his belt across his forehead to hold his head down, and to do it tightly to keep it from moving. I did, and then took off the leg brace to lift his legs higher in the air.

I held his nose again and began to suck. He couldn't move or wiggle. His arms were held fast with duct tape, his head was immobilized with the belt, and his torso was impaled on my cock. He was mine to ride, just like a motorcycle. I really started to fuck him fast now and sucked the air out of him like a fucking vacuum cleaner.

I had to allow him breaths in between, but they were quick and short and I covered his mouth quicker than he could catch his breath.

I was getting ready to bust a nut and I wanted to try and time mine with his. His eyes were glassy. He wasn't in the room with me, he was in some sort of fantasy . . . or relived nightmare. I lifted his hips up off the bed and pushed myself deep into him. With my free hand I grabbed his swollen mushroom head cock and held his mouth for the last time. I sucked and sucked and this time I went farther than I had before, I went deeper and deeper into his mouth and his ass. I could feel his dick start to spasm and the giz spurt out all over my hand. I lost it at this point and came deep inside him.

I collapsed on him and held him tight. He was breathing hard and so was I. I pulled out of him and untied his hands and head. We pulled in tight against each other and spooned, him in front of me. The finality of sex always leaves me sad and quiet, and I like to crawl away and slip into a stasis alone. This time was different. This time I held him in the silence. He lay in my arms and we were just two buddies who helped each other out. We each got what we needed.

In the morning the sunshine glinted on his helmet in a black and yellow glow. He put it on, lifted up the face shield, smiled, and winked his sad blue eyes at me. He revved his engine and took off down the street, back to the ship.

✯10✯ Under Officer

Brad

Varied popular and alternative media sources shaped my sexual fetish for military men. In my midteens I came across *The Report of the Commission on Obscenity and Pornography* (Bantam, 1970). In this richly illustrated government document, I discovered Tom of Finland's idealized graphic portrayals of bulging sailors and leather-clad Army officers. The arresting examples of his work made a profound impression on my emergent sexual desires and identity.

When I first started college at eighteen, a *Mother Jones* profile of gay veterans who had fought in World War II furthered my attraction. Subtler but no less erotically charged was an image in a photography book from my university library. Marie Cosindas' "Sailors" (1966) resonated with a quiet homoerotic fraternity and an intimacy lacking in Tom of Finland's ejaculatory *uebermenschen* tableaux. The soft-focus portrait of two bare-chested young sailors in a small furnished room in Key West, clad only in white trousers, hinted at a warm bond between them. I ached to be a third party with the couple, rather than a mere distant voyeur.

Films that fetishized sailors, ranging from Kenneth Anger's *Fireworks* (1947) and Fassbinder's *Querelle* (1982) to Eisenstein's *Battleship Potemkin* (1925) and even *South Pacific* (1958), reinforced a homoerotic archetype of young sailors bonding with innocence and hidden desires.

Collectively, these works helped foster my eroticization of uniformed men. No one in my immediate family ever served in the armed forces. My only exposure to authentic military men was limited to the few short late-summer days each year when Seattle was host to U.S. and foreign navy ships as part of the annual Seafair festival, an event celebrating the city's nautical history. I would quietly swoon at young men roaming the streets in pairs and small groups in pursuit of sex and entertainment, attired in their starched white uniforms with cropped hair, clean-shaven faces, and excited grins.

Yet this interest in military men did not surpass my primary fetish: men's underwear. If my attraction to uniformed men was a media-derived gay aesthetic, my underwear fetish reflected some incipient "gay sensibility" of the male body exposed. I developed this taste as early as my preteens, discovering a stimulating attraction to jock straps and briefer, European-style G-strings, bikinis, and thongs. Even at thirteen, I felt a strong desire to wear these various types of underwear, an urge I satisfied through mail-order purchases from the Ah Men catalog, a California-based forerunner to International Male.

A couple of years ago, I had the opportunity to combine these interests. It was sparked by an e-mail that read: "INTERESTED IN MEETING A NAVAL OFFICER, 34, 6' 1", 190, NEXT WEEK?"

It sounded very tempting. I instantly replied and quickly heard back from Officer Mike. We immediately began sharing secrets, recounting our private sexual histories, and exposing our fantasies. Our exchange was not merely a superficial online flirtation but rather an intimate Internet courtship. Officer Mike was planning on meeting up with me in Seattle during a work visit to the submarine base in Bangor, Washington. We were both anxious to share our thoughts before negotiating a rendezvous.

At the time we "met" electronically, I was very busy preparing to launch a major performance arts event. My schedule was not flexible enough to accommodate time-consuming traditional dating rituals. In my rare free moments I would occasionally peruse gay erotica Web sites dedicated to male underwear. One of particular interest to me featured a daily underwear survey, with results posted the very next day. Questions posed included type, color, and brand name of underwear preferred; respondent's age and physical description; and general personal comments. The survey results varied wildly from day to day in description and commentary. Almost all of the respondents included e-mail addresses in their postings, generating an online personals aspect to the site. Officer Mike's e-mail to me was inspired by his curiosity about the thong I described wearing in my own response to the daily survey.

Stirring with thoughts informed by years of exposure to iconic representations of sailors in film, fashion photography, visual art, and gay erotica, I saw in Officer Mike an intensely stimulating opportunity: to realize my fantasy of having sex with a real military man. Through his typed messages glowing from my computer screen, started forming an exciting mental picture of Officer Mike. His offer to meet aroused in me a whirlwind of heady thoughts and expectations rooted in my impressions of the mystique enveloping Navy men and their legendary proclivities for sexual exploration. Here was my chance to experience firsthand an adventure worlds apart from the cheaply available one-night stands I'd experienced through the gay bar scene milieu. Although friends tell me I'm "a catch," I had not been sexually active for nearly a year.

However, the more absorbed I became, pondering our imminent meeting, the more I was filled with trepidation. Would Officer Mike lure me into a trap of homophobic violence? I recalled media reports of gay sailors beaten and even killed by sailors from their own ships. When I wrote him of these fears, Officer Mike reassured me, explaining, "The Navy image does not fit the Navy reality. Most Navy people are not the brutes depicted in the media, in movies, and on television."

In fact, Officer Mike described himself as a romantic and suggested I arrange plans for dinner. After working up my confidence, I replied with arrangements. Feeling somewhat directionless regarding formal dating etiquette, I decided to buy Officer Mike a thong, much like the kind I sometimes wear. In retrospect, it was an odd decision, but, after all, he and I had become acquainted through a gay erotica Web site dedicated to men's underwear. I picked out a green silk thong for him at a local underwear retailer and asked the sales clerk to have it giftwrapped.

When I arrived to meet him, I was taken by surprise. Officer Mike was much different in person than the persona my imagination had sculpted during our electronic correspondence. He looked older than he described and dressed more conservatively than I anticipated, sporting a beige duster, carrying an umbrella, and topping off his ensemble with a country gentleman's cap. He looked like an East Coast accountant. This style of dress, however, conveyed an appearance that he, too, was potentially nervous about our arrangement, which gave me some pause to imagine his reaction to his present.

We shared a prix-fixe dinner at a relatively upscale restaurant that offered us the warmth and privacy for intimate conversation. He was impressed with my dining selection and appeared to grow more comfortable with me despite what seemed like an awkward arrangement for both of us. Our initial exchange felt like an interview, but after a few glasses of wine over a wonderful meal, I began to see Officer Mike in a personable light. We shared discussions about where we grew up, where we went to school, and our sexual experiences.

While not altogether a stranger to gay sex, Officer Mike turned out to be rather inexperienced. He was very keen on having sex with me, articulating a desire to give me head. As the evening had grown late, we talked about going out to dinner again the following night. When he dropped me off at my apartment, I had just enough courage from the wine to present him with his gift. He was truly surprised to receive a present, and one so handsomely wrapped. He was even more surprised to discover it was a silk thong.

He laughed, flushing with some embarrassment. He had never before received such a gift or even worn a thong. He was a garden-variety underwear guy: classic white briefs and boxers. To return the favor, as he felt somewhat enamored of me and my gesture, he gave me his cover—his Navy officer's cap, which looked brand new. He told me that the caps are expensive, but he would have no trouble replacing it. We made out for a short while then arranged a meeting for the next night.

It turned out he couldn't make dinner the second night, so we just had coffee. We talked for a few hours and, as we walked around town, I began to have that nervous and excitable sensation that dating someone new produces. In this instance, it was particularly exciting to become acquainted with a naval officer, given that our meeting seemed like a shot in the dark.

We stopped to share a few glasses of wine and divulged more sexual fantasies, experiences, and personal details. He was quite interested in what had attracted me to his initial e-mail and what I found erotically appealing about the military. I described my attraction to the hip-hugging dungarees sailors wear, as well as their crisp dress whites. I told him that I already owned the so-called "Dixie Cup" cap. He grinned at my impressions and fetishized account.

On the third night, we arranged dinner in my downtown neighborhood. I was particularly exhausted from my late nights and work producing the arts event, so our dinner was relatively quiet. Just when I thought our evening would be cut short prematurely, Officer Mike invited me back to the naval base in Bangor. I was hesitant from fatigue, but he talked me into it.

Instead of catching the ferry across Elliott Bay, we drove south to Tacoma and then north to the base—about eighty miles. I was so tired that I slept the entire way. I woke up just as we approached the base, which was enshrouded in heavy fog. Officer Mike cautioned me to be discreet. At the guard crossing, he flashed his identification card, and we were on the base without incident.

It felt very strange being there. We drove past the recreation complex, where Officer Mike said all the "gym bunnies" worked out as early as five in the morning, and past a cafeteria that included a bar. We fell quiet approaching the Travelodge-style Bachelor Officer Quarters. He parked his car, and we gathered our things to go inside. It was very quiet. My heart was racing, as I knew what to expect. Officer Mike had promised he had a surprise waiting for me inside.

He opened the door to his room. Its furnishings, too, resembled a Travelodge or other modest franchise motel. On one end was a credenza upon which perched a large television, and just opposite was a queen-sized bed flanked by bed stands and reading lamps. Officer Mike's luggage and clothes were scattered throughout the room.

We got settled, and he confided that, after I had given him the thong, he'd come back to his room that night and put it on. He had never experienced the heightened arousal of wearing such underwear before and almost immediately reached orgasm through the silk fabric. Unfortunately, it was the wrong size; it was a medium, and he wears a size extra large.

Officer Mike produced his surprise for me. It was a sailor's tropics uniform, so called because it is issued for summer. The uniform included a white short-sleeved shirt with matching white trousers. I was impressed. He asked me to try it on, and I did, as he admired me in the bathroom mirror. Beaming, he said that I looked like any number of young sailor men in the Navy.

We sat on the edge of the bed. He turned on the television, channel-flipping through the cable selection until he found MTV. Moments later, he leaned over to kiss me, and we started to make out. We gradually undressed and, once disrobed, he put on his new thong. Although not erect, he said he felt very aroused. He worked his way down into my pants and began giving me blow job. It was perhaps the longest blow job I've ever received, lasting upwards of forty-five minutes, yet his technique was lacking. I tried to reciprocate, demonstrating how to give head to yield the fullest and satisfying result. But he was still only moderately aroused. Ultimately, he performed again on me for a while and I finally came, unloading all over his face.

Exhausted, we cleaned up, and I took a shower before retiring. The alarm quickly disrupted our few short hours of pleasant sleep. I had to return to Seattle so that I could get to work on time. We drove through the base McDonald's for coffee and breakfast and and then had a long, quiet drive back to Seattle.

In retrospect, it was a bleary and fascinating adventure with Officer Mike. It was not the best sex I have enjoyed, but we had a good time given the situation, which was remarkably spontaneous and memorable, like a modest short film.

In an e-mail I received from Officer Mike a week later, he confided that he was married—to a lesbian also in the Navy—but emphasized that he'd had a very good time meeting me. He was pleased that I had allowed him the opportunity to have sex with another man, a fantasy he had harbored in secret for many years. The experience, he said, filled him with warm memories, but he asked me to not write to him again. He felt like his sex life with his wife was rejuvenated, for which he assured me his wife would be grateful. Could it be from the sexual pleasure he enjoyed from wearing a thong?

In the years since we met, I have not had another opportunity to have sex with anyone in the military, yet my attraction to men in uniform continues to grow. Perhaps I'll encounter another military man who shares my underwear fetish, and our passions will take us on a new adventure.

☆11☆ On the Money

Maynard

Trust Your Instincts

I picked up sailors for almost twenty years, in both Tennessee and California (I consider myself semiretired due to the base closures here in the Bay Area). During all of those years of cruising, I never tried to put the move on more than one guy at a time. Safety was the main concern. I always felt I was tough enough to handle one guy if he turned violent. More than one was just too dangerous. Besides, the guys I approached were usually experimenting and considered themselves straight . . . and based on what I learned about the Navy, they would never trust a buddy to keep his mouth shut, and news about a homosexual encounter could be all over the ship in no time.

Once in Alameda I broke my own rules and gave two guys a ride. One was drunk and quickly passed out in the backseat. The other was drinking from an open container and decided to bait me. He kept asking me if I wanted to suck his dick.

"You know you want it," he said. "So let's do it."

My instincts told me that this guy was probably a gay basher and was trying to get me to leave my car and go off with him so he could jump me. So I dumped him and his drunken buddy at the base gate. I'll never know for sure, but if my intuition was wrong, I'm really pissed.

"Sorry My Friend Messed up Your Apartment"

There was another occasion when I ignored my rules and picked up two sailors at once in the early morning hours. They needed a ride from San Francisco back to Treasure Island Naval Station. One guy was gorgeous and sober. The other was ugly and drunk. But the Navy's buddy system was in full force and the good-looking redhead was not going anywhere with me without his inebriated pal. So with Drunken Sailor asleep in my backseat, the handsome sailor and I made small talk as we headed across the Bay Bridge. Then he accepted my invitation to skip the Treasure Island exit and continue on to my place in Oakland where we could have another few beers and continue our conversation.

Soon after arriving at my apartment Drunken Sailor became uncontrollable. He kept trying to take part in our little party, but he was too intoxicated to form complete sentences. Then when he staggered to the bathroom to take a piss, he was too drunk even to stand up. He tried to support himself by hanging onto the shower curtain, and pulled the curtain rod right out of the wall.

Red proposed that we drive Drunken Sailor to the base. He said that after that he would come back alone.

Yeah, right, I thought to myself as we carried his buddy to my car. *Another one that got away.*

When we got to the base and my new friend escorted his pal to the barracks, I parked in the visitors' area just outside the gate and waited. And waited. Several times I turned on the ignition but then shut it off again. If he did come back, this guy would be worth the wait, and that instinct of mine kept telling me that he actually might.

He did.

On the ride back to my apartment, Red repeatedly apologized for his buddy's behavior. "I'm sorry my friend messed up your apartment. It's that kind of stuff that gives us sailors a bad name. . . ."

I politely accepted his apology as I sped down the freeway, thrilled that this great guy had kept his word and was now going home with me—alone.

Did he know I wanted to have sex with him? Boy, did he! One beer later, I made my offer, and he accepted a blow job.

Red was as nice as any man you could ever hope to meet. But, like most sailors, he was just passing through, and I never heard from him again.

"Since We Have Sex Every Time I See You, Maybe It's Time That I Call"

I have never been able to fully understand how straight men think when it comes to the psychological aspects of receiving a blow job. Even if the blow job is good (and I have never given a bad one), most guys who consider themselves straight end up ruining the mood afterward by overanalyzing the event. They always have to find something—anything, no matter how small—to create guilt. They seem to reason, "There's no way that something that feels so good can be good, so it must be bad, and that means I have to feel bad about feeling good." That type of socially induced thinking really made it difficult for me to provide *repeat* services to sailors, even when we both knew that we wanted it to happen.

Kevin was a perfect example. He was stationed at Naval Air Station Alameda in the early 1980s. He told me he was on an aircraft carrier, but our meetings never lasted long enough for me to learn many details about his life. But this I do recall: Kevin loved the way I sucked his dick. Each time I saw him walking down Webster Street, it automatically followed that he would duck into the XXX movie arcade and wait for me to join him in a booth to give him head.

Kevin was handsome in a "regular guy" way. He had brown hair. His body was muscular from head to toe, but not gym conditioned. Though he had a deep voice, his speech was always quiet and relaxed. Even with his Navy-issue glasses, he was a nice-looking young man with a traditional, unassuming boy-next-door appeal. Just everything about him seemed natural.

I first approached Kevin after noticing him walking the streets. When I invited him to join me in the movie arcade for a blow job, it seemed to be the natural thing for him to do.

We soon developed a routine that never varied. Every time I happened to encounter him on the street he would enter the arcade, carefully making sure that none of his Navy buddies saw him. Then he'd step into a booth, watching a movie until I came in.

He always let me do the work with his clothes. I'd slowly unbuckle his belt, open his jeans, pull them down over his thick, slightly hairy thighs, and then pull down his underwear, always the traditional white briefs.

His cock was thicker than average and always hard before I even touched it. Watching the movie, he would slowly start a rotating motion with his hips, moving his dick in and out of my mouth, hardly ever taking his eyes off the screen. After a few minutes, there'd be less rotating and more in-out thrusting. Finally, his hips would reach a certain tempo that I learned to recognize as the signal that Kevin was almost ready to pop. I would increase my rubbing action around his balls and the inside of his thighs. He seemed to really like that. I could read his movements like a book. Seconds before he was ready to come, I would stroke Kevin's calf muscles as I kneeled before him then put both my arms between his legs and spread them ever so slightly, causing his knees to bow outward just as his cock pulsed and squirted his sweet juice into my mouth.

Each time was exactly the same. I worked that boy like a well-oiled machine. It was clear to both of us that we were sexually in tune with each other and that we needed to explore our teamwork somewhere other than a cramped dark booth in a video arcade. But he wouldn't do it. After all, getting your dick sucked in a semipublic place does not officially make you "gay," Kevin—like so many other sailors—believed. But accepting an invitation to come up to my apartment was a whole different matter. Why, that could even be considered a date. And since he was straight, a date was another guy was out of the question.

I serviced Kevin more than ten times at that arcade over about a year. I repeatedly gave him my phone number and begged him to call me, if only to tell me when to meet him so we could enjoy each other on a regular schedule. But he just couldn't bring himself to arrange a meeting. It had to be random chance or nothing.

That is, until the one night when he finally did call. And—as random chance would have it—I was on the night shift at work and did not return home until many hours after he left the long-awaited message on my answering machine.

"Hi, this is Kevin. I guess it's time I called you so we can get together." There was a long pause. "Sorry you're not home."

I never saw him or heard from him again.

"Just What I Need . . . to Get Caught Doing This!"

One night in the mid-1990s I was driving around Alameda pining for the good old pre-AIDS days when men were men and sailors were always horny. Then it happened. A cute sailor actually accepted a ride from me to base. And in the few blocks' ride before we reached the gate, he also accepted my offer to share the six-pack of beer I had in the car.

"But I can't go too far," he told me. "In the morning we're going back to Washington."

NAS Alameda was already starting to stand down, and the sailors in town were steadily growing fewer and fewer. And there were fewer and fewer gay cruisers like myself operating along Atlantic Avenue—not at all like the good old days when we accounted for a fair percentage of the traffic between the base and Webster Street, driving back and forth, day and night, hoping to seduce some handsome Navy kid fresh from the farm or the streets of some faraway city.

Vincent turned out to be from the Seattle area, and coincidentally his ship was stationed near there. The Alameda visit was just a stopover. He seemed concerned about getting at least some sleep that night (it was already after 2:00 a.m. and he was headed to the base because the bars had closed). But he was friendly and prelubricated by a few beers, and he seemed pleased that I took an interest in him and offered not just more beer but also conversation.

Over the years I found that many sailors who agreed to spend time with me were motivated more than anything else by a desire for company and contact with someone in the civilian world. While sex was my main goal, for the sailor it was usually something unanticipated that "just happened."

Vincent and I parked in a civilian apartment complex parking lot across the street from base—literally a stone's throw away from the gate. We chatted for a while about his life. Then he announced that he had to take a piss. He stepped out of the car and walked over to the fence between the parking lot and the street to urinate.

I stepped out of the car too, but it wasn't a release of beer that I was seeking. I wanted to watch Vincent.

Until this point I had not directly approached the subject of sex and still had no idea if this nice-looking sailor from Seattle would even consider the possibility. But there we were. Only a thin wooden fence and a wide boulevard with a swath of grass in the center separating us from the guards at the gate: Vincent with his dick in his hand, I with lust in my heart.

Maybe Vincent instinctively knew what I wanted and hesitated before putting his treasure back into his pants. Or maybe I moved quickly and surprised him. I don't recall. But the next thing I knew I was kneeling beside him and reaching out to take his cock in my hand. He let me stroke it for a minute or so before he jumped back and said, "I'm not into that. Nothing personal against you." Why do they always say that?

We got back in the car and returned to our beers and our conversation. Only now the focus shifted to how I was attracted to him and how I loved to give pleasure to sailors and how I really hoped he would change his mind and let me suck his dick. I assured him there was no pressure (yeah, right) and I would only do what he wanted me to do, nothing else. After a little further discussion, he agreed that a blow job would be nice. I suggested that we get out of the car and go back over by the fence again so that no one could see us (unless some residents of the apartment complex walked into the parking lot—wouldn't they get a shock).

Vincent was nervous about being seen by the military police and expressed that concern as I went to work unsnapping his belt, opening his jeans, and pulling his pants and underwear to his knees. Usually I practice good blow job form by pulling the guy's pants all the way down to his ankles to allow more freedom of movement, but since there truly was a real possibility that we might have to cover up fast, the knees were good enough.

"This is just what I need . . . to get caught doing this," Vincent said almost to himself as he peered over at the base.

Despite the awkwardness of the situation and location, Vincent's cock was hard and ready. (Isn't youth wonderful?) I slowly licked and sucked his beautiful organ. His pleasing moans spoke volumes as he savored the head I was giving him. Finally, he did what all young men, straight, gay, or in between, have done since sex was discovered. As I held my head almost still, Vincent tensed his hips in that familiar fucking motion and pumped his cock into my face in a nice, steady rhythm, until he locked his jeans-covered knees and shot a sweet load of come down my throat.

He slumped back against the side of my car with a big grin on his face.

"How was that?" I asked.

"Great," he said. "I just can't believe I did that."

I didn't ask if he meant having man-man sex or doing it practically in front of the MPs. Vincent and I talked a little more before we both started yawning and decided to call it a night. He repeated how much he enjoyed the experience. I suggested that even though he was straight he should try to find a buddy who would be willing to suck his cock. He said he'd consider it.

"Good night," I said as he headed across the street to the base entrance.

He replied, "Good night. It was nice to meet ya."

Just then a woman from the apartment complex came strolling into the parking lot heading for a nearby car. Timing is everything.

On the Money

I never kidded myself thinking that every military guy I ever sucked did me because of my charm or looks. There were many who did me because they were horny and any mouth would do. Any port in a storm, as they say. There were also some who did it for the money.

I have no problem with that, as long as both parties understand and accept the nature of the customer-client exchange from the beginning. I would much rather see a handsome young man using his body in a safe manner to raise funds instead of turning to robbery or some other violent crime. Over the years I have slipped many a sailor or soldier ten, twenty, thirty, forty, or fifty dollars in exchange for the pleasure of sucking his dick.

One such encounter occurred on vacation in San Diego. For me, sightseeing there meant looking at a lot of palm trees, a lot of zoo animals, and a lot of XXX arcades scattered around town frequented by sailors and Marines. (This particular visit occurred in the mid-1980s, before some local politician decided to have all the doors removed from arcade booths.)

Except for the trade aspect, the encounter was pretty standard. I was cruising the arcade, hungry for sailor cock. A cute redheaded young Navy man entered. He looked around, looked at me, then stepped into a booth.

I quickly followed. He explained that he was short on cash and needed to make ten bucks so that he could rejoin his friends at some bar down the street. I had already unbuckled his belt before the words "Sure, no problem," crossed my lips. This beautiful guy could have asked for ten times that amount. (I might not have had $100 in my wallet, but he could have asked.) He was even a little sheepish about asking me to provide all the quarters for the movies. I slowly worked on his uncut cock until he rewarded me with his cream and I rewarded him with twenty dollars. (He deserved more than the ten he had requested.) We hugged briefly in the tiny booth before he squeezed by me and out the door.

Another encounter involved Mike, a soldier stationed at the Fort Ord Army post on the Monterey Peninsula. I came across him two times and both times we were supposed to have a trade. But both times he left without the cash.

The first time I saw Mike was in North Beach as he stood outside a dance club next door to an XXX video arcade. Mike had apparently decided to try his hand at making a little extra money while his buddies were inside the club trying to pick up girls. I don't think he was very good at male hustling. After he let me follow him into a video booth I was already on my knees and his pants were already falling to his shoe tops before he broached the prospect of being paid for what I was already doing. It's not polite to talk with your mouth full, and since my mouth was full of his dick I simply didn't acknowledge the request for money. He came after only a few minutes of sucking.

I explained to Mike that I didn't have much money on me. This was true. I promised to make it up to him the next time I saw him.

The next time was months later, at the same place. I honestly intended to honor the promise I'd made Mike. However, there was a distraction. A female prostitute—one of the few actually bold enough to openly solicit in touristy North Beach—was brazenly working the sidewalk in front of the one XXX arcade where the clerks were too lazy to kick her out. Just as I approached Mike about trade, the hooker was hauling a sailor into the arcade. This I had to see. I gambled that Mike would patiently bear with me when I told him there was something I needed to take care of in the arcade before I could go to the bank to get the money for our transaction. He agreed to wait. I hurried into the arcade and was lucky enough to find an empty booth next to the one occupied by the hooker and her sailor trick.

Many of these booths have small holes drilled in the walls, the work of gay cruisers who enjoy peeping in on men who masturbate behind locked doors. I've never drilled a peephole in all my years of cruising, but I'm a frequent user. That night I used one to watch the sailor fuck the prostitute, doggy-style, standing up. She didn't even give the guy any head as foreplay. She just stroked his already hard cock a couple of times, then turned her back to him and asked if he was ready to put it in.

Do you have to ask? I felt like saying.

While she contemplated her grocery list or something, he pumped about five times, pulled out, and came on her butt.

I shook my head sadly. *Sailors pay good money for sex this poor?* I thought, and I hoped I'd have a chance to catch this guy and offer him a much better orgasm, free of charge. But the sailor left with the hooker.

I left to look for Mike, who was not waiting outside as he promised. In fact, he was nowhere to be found. I truly intended to keep my word on our trade agreement. I guess he didn't believe me.

"Can You Help Me with This?"

My favorite sailor-hustler of all time was Rick. He was another guy off one of the ships based at Alameda. He was cute with a mop of curly blond hair and a lanky, almost hairless body, but behind his boyish good looks he was very street smart.

I first met Rick by offering him a ride. It didn't take long for him to accept my invitation to spend time together. He was very forthright and explained that he could use some extra money and asked if I could provide that.

Rick and I developed an understanding that we could get together sometimes and I would be happy to provide some cash. But he also understood that I was just an average working guy and that he could not get greedy. So Rick would call me occasionally and we'd have a good time with each other. Part of the fun was that he was not cold like many male hustlers can be. Perhaps you've met the type, where sex is purely business and not enjoyment, and they are angry with themselves—and therefore angry with you—for having to do the things they do. Often with male hustlers, sex has no soul.

Rick was not like that at all. He and I had a lot of fun. He genuinely seemed to enjoy being with me, and he loved to hang around at the apartment and do other things together like spontaneously hit the bars in Oakland or grab some dinner. The money was almost an afterthought. There was one occasion when I explained that I could not afford to pay him and he wanted to come over to my place anyway.

Rick was sitting on the living-room floor watching TV. I was in another room doing something else.

"Hey, Maynard. Can you come in here and help me with this?"

When I walked in the room there he was with his big, hard cock sticking out of his shorts.

"Go for it," he told me.

You hear a lot of nonsensical talk about the size of male sex organs. Just read any porno book from cover to cover and it'll have you believing that the average dick size is nine to ten inches. What bullshit. I've serviced a lot of men for more than twenty years and watched a lot of others through peepholes as they jacked off. Six or seven inches is the norm. Occasionally you may see an eight. In Rick's case, the lad really was blessed. He really did sport about eight or nine inches. It was nice and fat and uncut, with a big bulb of a head. My love of men and their cocks has nothing to do with penis size. But his dick really was quite a sight, big and hard, sticking out at an upward curve from his lanky, almost skinny body.

Rick was something special. But, like all the sailors I've encountered, one day he just vanished. And I was not surprised when I didn't hear from him anymore.

However, that was not the end of the story.

About a year after the last time we got together, I once again went cruising my favorite adult movie arcade in North Beach. One of my "friends," a fellow cruiser who was well aware of my "taste for seafood," told me there was a sailor locked inside one of the booths. Other cruisers had tried and failed to get the sailor to open the door, so they were resigned to just peeping through the hole in the wall and watching him play with himself. When they got the chance, that is. Not all of the cruisers were on friendly terms, and one snotty queen was monopolizing the booth next to the sailor.

Don't ask me why, but when I jiggled the doorknob of the sailor's booth, he suddenly opened it. There were two sounds: one was the door locking behind me as I rushed in. The other was a crash in the neighboring booth as Snotty Queen fell from the bench to the floor in shock, horror, and envy. The young man's beautiful dick was sticking out of his pants and I was on my knees just about to take it in my mouth when he said, "Hey, Maynard."

To my shock, it was Rick. I had failed to recognize him in the dark room (plus my main focus was on his crotch, not his face). Before I could even say anything there was a loud pounding on the door.

The arcade clerk yelled, "Only one person allowed per booth!"

It was hardly news to the clerks that men went into booths together, but usually they never bothered you unless someone complained. This particular clerk, however, had been paid off by Snotty Queen to satisfy his jealous rage by harassing me and hopefully scaring off the sailor and ruining my good fortune.

I turned to Rick and said, "Let's go."

He smiled. "Sure."

We walked out past everyone with big grins on our faces. As Rick and I headed down the sidewalk toward my car, I looked back to see cruisers, both friendly and hostile, standing outside the arcade staring in astonishment. You could have knocked Snotty Queen over with a feather.

Tough Love

I guess we all look back on the best sex we ever had and we remember it as such for a variety of reasons. Of all the sailors in my life, first prize goes to a guy I met in a downtown Memphis XXX arcade back when I was in my early twenties. He was, to put it mildly, not interested at first.

I was cruising the arcade when this strapping guy about my age came in. He had short dark hair, wore about a day's growth of beard, and was just under six feet tall. I followed him around, but he looked mean and it seemed like he did not want to be bothered. He went into a booth and left the door unlocked. I was afraid to try anything. Then he came out and went to another booth. I took that as a sign that he might actually be cruising too, so I tried the door. It was unlocked. I gathered up my courage, opened the door, and walked in on him. I wasn't inside the booth for five seconds before he grabbed me, slammed me against the wall, got right in my face, and said, "Get the fuck out!"

I guessed that meant he was not interested after all.

Rejected and dejected, I went back to standing around and shopping for other prospects. The cute guy continued to periodically move from booth to booth. We avoided eye contact, but my body language made it clear that I wanted him in the worst way. I boldly went over and tried the door again. Unlocked. I again mustered my courage, cracked the door open, and sheepishly looked in. No movement at all from Cute Guy. I slipped into the booth, standing by the door with my hand on the knob, ready to make a fast getaway. Still no reaction. I asked him if I could stay. No response. I stayed. Clearly, he wanted me. Cute Guy sat quietly as I reached over to rub his leg . . . and then his crotch. This was it. I motioned for him to stand up as I went to my knees. Down came his pants, down came his shorts, and I proceeded to give him head. After a while, he blew a load.

He still didn't say much, but I took the opportunity to invite him over to my apartment so we could continue to get acquainted. He accepted. He followed me home in his pickup truck. I was surprised, all the more so since it was a ten-mile drive from downtown to where I lived.

When we arrived at my place John introduced himself. He apologized for the rough treatment he gave me at first. He offered no explanation for it. He said he decided he was curious about gay sex and this was a good time to give it a try.

Sounded good to me. We relaxed and moved to the bedroom to undress. The evening had certainly already offered up more than I could have hoped, but there were more surprises to come. I figured since this was John's first time with another man, the sex would follow the usual pattern for this situation: I would give him more head and he would lie there and enjoy it but not offer to reciprocate in any way. I was pleasantly surprised when he became very affectionate and responded by doing to me all the things that I was doing to him. He even kissed. We were completely in sync sexually.

I will never forget the two of us lying on our sides, face to face. I lifted one of his legs and slowly fucked his butt. After I came, without changing positions, he lifted one of my legs and slowly fucked me. I can still see his face, smiling with his eyes closed when he muttered under his breath, "Oh baby," as he came and shot his load into me.

It was truly perfect sex, with perfect give and take.

When John got up to go, heading back to Millington, north of Memphis, it dawned on me that he was in the Navy. The regulation military haircut in an era when short hair was uncommon should have been an immediate giveaway. But this encounter was before I started specifically targeting sailors for sex.

I'm glad that I can now look back and vividly remember how one of my most memorable sexual experiences ran the gamut of emotions—starting out rough, ending with perfect gentleness—and involved a military man who chose not to let a golden opportunity pass him by.

☆12☆

Trouble Loves Me

Steven Zeeland

Handsome young sailors half my age seduced me, gave me drugs, and pressured me to videotape them performing lewd acts.

I never wanted to make a porn video. It happened by accident. With some help from the ghost of a beefcake photographer. . . .

I know it sounds farfetched.

Running a background check on me will not likely make my claim appear any more immediately credible. My record includes authoring several books that could at first glance be mistaken for porn. Especially *Military Trade,* the cover of which depicts a nude Marine. And in various interviews I've called myself a "military chaser."

But only for want of a better term.

To the extent that I have it in me to be at all a predator, I have always ended up captured by the game.

Bremerton, Washington—January 2001: Navy Stray Cat Blues

"Dude, I really need to jerk off."

I turn my head to meet the sailor's eye. But he suddenly looks worried at what he's just said and doesn't give me a chance to comment before hastily adding, "Hey, you don't mind me calling you 'dude'?"

Pro and I are lying on separate parallel couches, watching DVD porn on my living-room TV.

I feign a frown. "No . . ."

Pro's accent is so subtle I don't really think of him as a Texan. But it occurs to me that back where he comes from young men still say "ma'am" and "sir." And that maybe he just now remembered that the year he was born I graduated high school.

"Why would I mind you calling me 'dude'?"

But before he can open his mouth I tell him that if he wants any lube, in the cabinet next to the TV he'll find three different varieties, and I add which brand I use.

Pro's preferences are not the same as mine. But he doesn't take offense at my using a petroleum-based lubricant.

Pro likes his lube slick and water-soluble. And the fleshtone pixels he studies on my monitor are of a different body type.

My own gaze is less focused, intermittently shifts offscreen, and especially during the longer super slow-mo intervals unabashedly favors his body.

Pro's body is flawless. His face is more handsome than any in my straight-porn DVD collection. He doesn't mind being admired with his shirt off and his jeans around his ankles.

But Pro isn't a hustler. And though the first time he visited me I paid him a respectable hourly rate for a test shoot in my studio, tonight he's not here as a model. We're just hanging out. My high-resolution digital camera is on the coffee table right next to me, and that's where it stays the whole time Pro masturbates. Until, that is, the very end.

"I'm just about there, dude."

"Pro, uh, do me a favor?"

A pause. Then, a low, flat, "What?"

I'm pretty sure I know what he's thinking. Something along the lines of *What the fuck? I should have known . . . And just when I thought—Or maybe? God, I hope it's pictures of the money shot he wants.*

But one extraordinary quality I've already noted in Pro is his inimitable knack for shattering the ordinary. At random intervals, sufficiently infrequent to defy prediction yet somehow uncannily precisely timed, he'll do or say something so off the wall as to utterly floor you. But so casually, and so adroit and so fleeting, that in the second it takes you to register and look to his face for some sort of accounting, you find yourself confounded by "the neutral face of the Buddha" (which is far and away the only trait of the insatiably desiring Pro even remotely suggestive of the Buddha). And Pro, for his part, has already declared his admiration for my own offbeat "edge."

"I think we need to do something symbolic to mark this night. Would you mind ejaculating on my TV screen?"

Pro almost manages to not smile. "Are you sure?"

The monitor in question is a new, pricey, flat-screen Sony. A gift from a patron.

"Yes. I want to photograph your semen dripping down the screen."

Pro gives my TV a copious "facial." After he leaves the room to wash up I snap three shots and stare at the screen speculatively, wondering how much this AWOL sailor's spunk would taste of the strychnine-rich methamphetamine he shared with me twelve hours ago (my first experience with street drugs since the 1980s).

Pro steps back into the room.

"Dude, when are you going to finally make a video of me? I'm serious. We need to do this. I wanna be in porn, man!"

☆ ☆ ☆

I see this anecdote hasn't strengthened my case any. How can I claim to be an "accidental pornographer" when I have all *the equipment?*

The first time Pro visited my studio, he thought out loud: "You actually have strobe lights."

And what *legitimate* business could I have residing in a Navy shipyard ghetto devoid of any diversions save for sailors and seedy bars? It may be possible to accept an author of global ultramarginal cult standing not opting for New York or Los Angeles. But it's rather more difficult to concede much leeway to a vegetarian nondriver who opts to dwell where the only restaurant within walking distance is McDonald's and still claims he's not there for "military meat."

Ah, but here's where my story gains some credibility, if only as a potential insanity defense: You see, I moved to this isolated Navy ghost town—where it rains even more than in neighboring Seattle—from San Diego, California, "military chaser" central, USA. And military porn video central.

And I fled to escape my apprenticeship in military beefcake photography.

☆ ☆ ☆

San Diego, California—January 1996: Pornographer's Apprentice

Rewind five years.

I'm in the passenger seat of a cheap leased car, very slowly puttering through a mountainous stretch of San Diego County east toward the desert. Behind the wheel is a man of advanced years and failing health. His breath is rancid. He's subject to wild mood swings. He recites the same anecdotes and same old jokes with trying frequency, and rarely betrays the faintest interest in listening to anyone else. But for once, I've managed to catch and hold his attention, reading aloud to him from *The New Yorker*.

It's Susan Faludi's "The Money Shot," the part about the porn video former U.S. Marine John Wayne Bobbitt starred in to exhibit his surgically reattached penis.

David guffaws so loudly, is so delighted by the story that I'm almost stoked. And mistakenly imagine that David might share my interest in Faludi's cultural commentary on how ejaculating onscreen in porn video has supplanted more traditional demonstrations of masculine prowess such as working in a shipyard. Only a discharge of David's intestinal gas prompts me to glance over and realize that he's no longer paying the slightest attention.

"I've decided to send her my galleys for *The Masculine Marine,*" I conclude. "I know it's a long shot. Probably we won't end up meeting over arugula and bottled water in LA. But a blurb from Susan Faludi—"

David looks at me intently. He nods, indicating the landscape to our left. "I've often wondered," he intones, "how those rocks got there."

Well, it's less of a non sequitur than it was twenty-four hours ago, when he made the same pronouncement at the same spot. . . .

☆☆☆

This is day two of my new part-time job, assisting David Lloyd on outdoor nude photo shoots of straight military men.

Yesterday the model was a brawny Coast Guardsman named Andy who chattered nervously the entire two hours it took us to reach the desert. On the ride there he was too polite—or scared—to comment on David's failure to observe the minimum speed limit and only once said, "Your turn signal's still on."

He did however put his foot down when David at last stopped the car and declared, "This is the place."

David's "ravine backdrop" was directly astride the highway and in clear view of the highway and its near-constant parade of retirees in RVs, who, confused by the fork in the road there, drove as slowly as David.

The Coast Guardsman balked.

I suggested, "Maybe just behind those rocks?"

David grimaced darkly. He raised his arms like a Joshua tree and bellowed, "There goes half the day right there!" We climbed fifty paces farther into the scrub.

At the conclusion of the shoot as we were packing up to leave Andy got some horrible cactus thing embedded in his foot and made a big deal of stoically yanking it out, for my benefit.

He was less stoic on the ride home, however, when David, in the thrall of another rambling stock narrative, momentarily mistook the treacherous two-lane mountain highway for Interstate 5 and drifted into the other lane. There were shouts, imprecations, and then apologies from Andy.

"Man! I'm sorry I grabbed the wheel. But you just missed hitting that car! We would have been dead! Man, you scared me!"

David graciously forgave him. Glancing at me in the rearview mirror, he rolled his eyes at this studly straight guy's nervous nelly attack.

Today's model is a Marine. Because he's stationed north of San Diego at Camp Pendleton, he drives his own car to a rendezvous point on the edge of the desert.

Kris is of Scandinavian ancestry. He fits certain of my stereotypes of Marines and Scandinavians. Kris is so reserved that even David runs out of banter.

And when David pulls over to his ravine backdrop directly astride the highway, Kris evinces a European absence of inhibition. David hands him the girlie magazine and we simply stand there as Kris casually works up a hard-on. By the second roll Kris has clambered onto a high rock and in plain view of passing cars swings his enormous erection. Chortling, David produces a ruler and measures it. "By God!" he roars. "Eight and three-quarter inches! That's how big Mr. Smiley is!"

Pleased with the $500 he's just pocketed, Kris is slightly less taciturn on the ride back. Thinking of Susan Faludi, I ask him whether he sees any potential connection between having proven his masculinity in the Marine Corps and modeling.

"No. You can get into a lot of trouble doing this."

I realize I'm receiving instruction here: being rebellious and naughty is almost as much reward as money and attention.

☆ ☆ ☆

As a third-generation Dutch American from suburban Grand Rapids, Michigan, with a Calvinist-cum-fundamentalist upbringing, I am not altogether dissimilar to Kris in terms of social restraint. This, I know, is a quality of mine that David values. To the extent I find the experience of witnessing more or less perfect physical specimens of the U.S. Armed Forces stripping and performing indecent acts sexually arousing, I don't betray it. Still, when David calls me up a few days later and reports that at the conclusion of a second, studio, shoot Swedish Marine Kris requested and was granted permission to ejaculate, I almost feel left out.

David had no choice but to reshoot Kris—hastily. All eight rolls of film he shot in the desert were overexposed beyond salvation.

Even on his best days, David has to shoot double or triple the number of images any other photographer would owing to his shaky hands. Tremor is a common side effect of lithium, the medication David takes for his bipolar disorder.

David is puzzled as to why this should be so much more a problem outdoors than in the studio. When I ask him why he doesn't just use a faster shutter speed, he's at a loss to answer. It's never occurred to him to toy with the automatic settings on his Nikon, he confesses.

"I don't have time!"

David earns upward of $100,000 a year from his photography. His work has been published in virtually every gay skin magazine at home and abroad and is endlessly recycled in phone-sex ads and other second-use outlets. Who am I to tell him about f-stops?

"The shoot was a total loss!" he thunders, with such outrage and wonder you'd think he'd just witnessed a cloud of locusts descending on San Diego specifically intent on devouring his Agfachromes of the Swedish Marine's "Mr. Smiley." "But I still had to pay Kris the same money again. *In cash!*" In a quieter tone he thinks to add, "And of course you'll still get your check."

I know that when David does pay me it's as much for my company as anything. And he knows that I wouldn't help him sort through slides or type up correspondence for fifteen dollars an hour if I didn't enjoy hearing his stories.

And as outrageous as his demands sometimes are, I somehow still feel terribly guilty when I nervously announce to David that my roommate Alex Buchman is thinking of moving to Seattle.

He sees through me in an instant. "You are not seriously thinking of moving to Seattle!"

He looks more crestfallen than I anticipated. Given the one-sidedness of our exchanges, I don't like to think that David sees something of himself in me. It's easier to focus on his sighs about how hard it will be to find another assistant like me—someone he can carry on a conversation with *and* who "doesn't drool" over big-dicked Marines.

David grew up in Seattle. His final word is, "I give it two years, three at the most. You're not a Seattle kind of guy." Nodding with conviction he turns his head away and pronounces, "You'll be back."

☆ ☆ ☆

Bremerton, Washington—January 1999: Stiffed

Two years later *Military Trade* is almost off press. David is one of the "military chasers" interviewed. One of his naked Marines is on the cover.

But David suffers a massive stroke and dies some months before I write my English friend Mark Simpson that I've realized I'm not really a Seattle kind of guy. "Since I can't seem to face returning to San Diego, I think I might as well take advantage of being perhaps the only person in Seattle who can move to Bremerton without losing face."

Bremerton, Washington, is a downscale Pacific Northwest town located between the similarly depressed hometown of Kurt Cobain (Hoquiam/Aberdeen) and Seattle, with no Starbucks and only one employer, the U.S. Navy shipyard.

I'm drawn to an old brick apartment building of institutional appearance. Only after I move in do I learn that it was constructed during World War I as an annex to the Navy Yard Hotel.

The last time Bremerton flourished was World War II. Most of the storefronts are boarded up. But there are a lot of churches. And taverns.

Bremerton is notorious for its population of sexually aggressive women—"Fat chicks chasin' fellas in the Navy," in the offensive words of Seattle rapper Sir Mix-A-Lot's 1987 song "Bremelo."

I've never lived "on the wrong side of the tracks" before. By the end of my first week here I'm starting to feel a little creeped out. Walking through town I'm struck by the number of burned-out houses posted ARSON. REWARD. I pick up the local paper and read that a woman was raped in the parking lot below my bedroom window. A Friday evening crawl of waterfront bars leaves me struggling to picture myself fitting in here at all.

I'm about to give up for the night when I pass by a derelict tavern and notice that there are lights on inside. The door is open. I walk in and am immediately greeted, "Steve!" A gay submariner recognizes me from a book reading.

The Crow's Nest dates back a century. Knowing that Bremerton is too small and too working class to sustain a gay bar, the new owner aims for an unobtrusively gay-friendly mixed bar. Reopening night, the crowd is engagingly motley. There are more gay submariners, there are Bremelos—and on the barstool to my right there is a drunken bug-eyed misfit who announces that he is self-publishing a chapbook of poems about crossing Bremerton ferry.

"Steve writes about fairies too," remarks my submariner friend.

The DVD plays George Michael's "Outside" video. Just below the monitor, an old wooden placard reads:

WELCOME ABOARD.
THE LORD TAKES CARE OF DRUNKS AND SAILORS.

I find myself making eye contact with a sailor. When he goes to the men's room, I follow. But I don't get to stand next to him at the awkwardly intimate urinals—someone else beats me to it. Peeing next to the sailor is a thirtyish man sporting short hair and a golf cap. With aching clarity I overhear him inquire, "So . . . are you in the Navy?"

When the sailor leaves the bar, I somehow feel obliged to sidle up next to the luckless chaser.

He's startled, even shocked that I've pegged him. Buddy tells me that he doesn't like gay culture, he just likes guys. I mention an English writer friend who's edited a book called *Anti-Gay* and his invitation to take me to Plymouth.

"Oh. I've been to Plymouth. It's like Bremerton. I mean, it's a lot bigger. But," Buddy shakes his head, "they've got the same Bremelos."

☆ ☆ ☆

I become a regular at the Crow's Nest. A sailor I meet there becomes something of a boyfriend. When he's out to sea, I hang out with Buddy. By summer we're drinking pals.

And what a summer it is. Weekend nights the bars are packed with sailors off the USS *Abraham Lincoln,* an aircraft carrier in town for a six-month overhaul. Buddy and I make a game of compiling weekly top-ten lists of our favorites. Even though—he is anxious that I understand this—he cannot himself be termed a military chaser. He's not a predator. "And," he reasons, "I also like firemen."

I don't disabuse Buddy of his conviction that he doesn't fit any stereotypes. And indeed, it seems that the only people who perceive Buddy as stereotypically gay are visiting urban gays.

I accompany Buddy on his nearly nightly rounds of the roughest dive bars on the waterfront. Buddy plays pool with sailors. I sit on bar stools and listen to career Navy alcoholics' sea stories.

These guys tend to come from small towns in the southern United States—or neighboring Idaho. Young men who never once jump on the ferry to Seattle by themselves, because they never have. Instead, they booze and brawl alongside the Bremelos.

Buddy takes to introducing me to local people as a "famous author"—a title that calls for too much explanation. One night I adjure my drinking pal, "Don't tell people I'm a famous author. Tell them I'm a famous photographer."

I'm half-joking. The only photos I've had published are in my own books. But among the thousands of *Lincoln* sailors, a half dozen or so who have become "downtown" regulars exude indisputable star quality, and one night it becomes more than I can bear.

We're in Buddy's favorite bar. I'm entertaining an out-of-town dignitary, a professor at one of the military academies. The prettiest of the *Lincoln* boys is there—drinking Bud by the pitcher, playing pool, and stealing the hearts or at least admiring glances from everyone present. He's winsome beyond measure, from his disarming constant grin to his tight Wrangler jeans to the heavily autographed cast on his broken arm. An inscription jumps out at me:

DON'T JERK OFF SO HARD

Buddy and the professor are merely charmed. And as for me . . .

When yet another young sailor staggers in, spots Castboy and with unstudied passion immediately throws his arms tightly around him, I get all misty-eyed, struggle to recite Whitman, and drunkenly vow that I will not return to this bar without a camera because "That picture would have been worth more than all of my books put together."

Buddy is keen on the idea but cautions me that before I start taking any pictures of sailors in the bar a protocol must be devised. I should wait until the hour when everyone is a little drunk but not yet sloppy drunk. The first pictures must be of people we know—say, Buddy and a woman, and then with some other guy. And only then take pictures of a sailor, but still only with a girl.

"If anybody gives you trouble, I'll back you up."

There was trouble, all right. But not like Buddy expected.

The first night I worked up enough nerve to pop my electronic flash in a waterfront pool hall a sailor angrily confronted me: "Why are you taking pictures of him instead of me?"

Of course I obliged him. But this angered the sailor I had been taking pictures of. Losing the spotlight, he sulked. Seeing this, I reassured him, "Well, don't let it go to your head, but you definitely have the most potential as a model." That was Mike, the sailor with the cast on his arm.

When his best friend from the ship walked in, Mike proudly repeated my appraisal.

This sailor in turn took me aside and demanded, "Him? You're wasting your film. Dude! His ears are too big!" And that was Packard, the sailor who would end up starring in *Out of the Brig,* the porn video I made by accident.

Bremerton, Washington—Summer 1999: Trouble Loves Me

As with any accident, memory blurs. This much is known:

That summer *Honcho* ran an interview with me to promote *Military Trade*. When I e-mailed the editor my thanks, I attached some JPGs of sailors drinking and playing pool. Doug McClemont wrote back that he liked the pictures. He invited me to shoot a few rolls of slide film for publication in his magazine.

At the time, I didn't own any strobe lights (much less any video equipment).

Of the three USS *Lincoln* sailors who'd fought over who was the most photogenic, one was in the brig and another was in a military treatment center for substance abuse. When I relayed *Honcho*'s invitation to Packard, he expressed skepticism. "Yeah, but how much would it pay?"

I told him how much.

Packard may or may not have dropped his pool stick. It seems like it was only a matter of hours before I'd shot enough rolls of Kodak EPP to FedEx to New York and woke up to a voice mail from Doug telling me the pictures were okay—only, "They're a little dark. If you can, try to get just a basic monolight."

For once, I wasn't "in between books." I had the money, but what motivated me to spend $1,000 on basic studio lighting equipment was not the promise of selling more layouts. I wanted to spare my models the shame of telltale amateur shadows.

That summer the (beefy but reclusive) Navy master-at-arms living next door to me vacated his one-room apartment. I toyed with the extravagant idea of renting the "studio," but not seriously—until the building manager accepted a rental application for the unit from a Bremelo with two small children.

"Well, I'll have the linoleum replaced for you." My landlady was perplexed but also impressed at my renting two apartments. "And about the cracks in the walls—"

She didn't argue when I told her I liked the room exactly as it was.

I had sense enough not to gush about how especially fond I was of the vintage Murphy bed and its stained mattress. Instead, I asked her what she knew about how the building had been furnished during World War II when it served as officers' quarters.

After I dragged up from the basement a battered chair and matching nightstand, my studio was ready. In the thirteen months I rented it I didn't change a detail.

That summer I was prescribed Paxil (paroxetene), an antidepressant/antianxiety drug in the same family of selective serotinin reuptake inhibitors as Prozac. Overall, the medication made me more self-assured and confident. Bold, even. I would not have dived into neophysique photography without it.

Paxil also abated some of my anxieties about turning into David Lloyd.

But one side effect of Paxil resulted in a new and unwelcome physical resemblance to David. From my first video recording made in the new studio:

PACKARD: I can see why you like the "steady shot" feature so much.

ZEELAND: [mock confrontationally] So what are you trying to say?

PACKARD: I can see your hands shaking right now.

ZEELAND: [Remains silent]

PACKARD: [Coughs and looks away]

The camcorder was an impulse purchase, prompted by cues from sailors I spoke with about modeling. The most succinct and memorable:

"So . . . you only take *still* pictures?"

It was in answer to another magazine editor's invitation that I became acquainted with videomaker Dink Flamingo of ActiveDuty.com. At the close of my interview with him for *Unzipped* Dink confided that he'd never aspired to become a pornographer. His ambition had always been to be a journalist.

We agreed to "trade places for a day." Dink promised to contribute some authentic accounts of erotic liaisons with "barracks bad boys" to Alex Buchman's nonfiction anthology in progress. I pledged to try my hand at playing auteur in his scandal-ridden, sordid "adult amateur video" subgenre.

After patiently bearing with me for nine long months, Dink breathed satisfaction and relief upon receipt of the labor of love I finally delivered.

My timing, however, could not have been worse. The scheduled release date for my video celebrating real-life military deserters coincided with the bombings of the World Trade Center and the Pentagon.

Still, my three masturbating sailors cannot really be accused of "disgracing the military." The title *Out of the Brig* is no fantasy; it's documentary. The sailors in it are real-life tattooed Navy "bad boys" who really have broken the rules, have done their time, and are no longer on active duty—are no longer answerable to anyone. (Even if at the scheduled release date one of them had not yet turned himself in. Had Congress officially declared war, and had he been arrested, he could have faced the firing squad.)

Barracks Bad Boys: *The Movie*

The style of my directorial debut is a cross between early Dirk Yates and early Andy Warhol. With, I'd like to think, a human face.

But not mine.

FIRST SAILOR: Approximately three minutes into the opening sequence, which stars Packard, you can hear me say: "You know, you could even sort of self-direct this" (as I hand him a second remote, and flip over the camcorder viewfinder so that he can zoom in and out to . . . self-direct).

SECOND SAILOR: After a short introductory scene (unscripted and shot in one take at a retro adult video arcade just outside the shipyard), I don't do much "directing." This one stars Pro. He masturbates watching DVDs on my living-room TV.

THIRD SAILOR: The first two sequences are exactly twenty minutes long. The closing sequence is a film within a film, and a full hour long. It's an essay by itself, too. For my purpose here, it's enough to tell you that I miscalculated in thinking that for this shoot I had an assistant who would effectively play "Steve" to my "David." But when the door to my own studio slammed shut with me locked out, I was surprised but not altogether displeased.

And when an hour and a half later I was allowed back in the room and rewound through some of the tape, I knew that this was it. My "sailors gone bad" had given me enough "raw footage" to meet the basic requirements of the amateur military porn video idiom. Now I could give myself over to endless hours lovingly *editing*.

Bremerton, Washington—January 2003

By the time you read this I will no longer be in Bremerton, Washington. Every last one of the active-duty sailors I photographed has long since departed. Two or three of them transferred to distant duty stations; two or three received honorable discharges. Between twenty and thirty were kicked out of the Navy for "unauthorized absence" and/or drug use. In February 2002, the Navy announced that all of the ships currently homeported in Bremerton would be moved elsewhere. Also, that the block of 100-year-old buildings adjacent to the Navy shipyard—including the historic Crow's Nest tavern—would be demolished to provide a "security buffer" against terrorist attack. But the bar shut down even before the wrecking ball hit, after the thirty-seven-year-old owner was found dead under mysterious circumstances.

Pro has long since moved back to Texas. But he's kept in touch. And at one point when I was too long in replying to his e-mail he left me a voice mail:

"Steve! Come out of your fucking Pax-hole!"

Actually, I'd quit Paxil and sworn off maintenance drugs of any sort just before September 11, 2001.

"Are we still friends or what? Dude! *I shot my seed on your TV!*"

It isn't very often I turn on my TV, and almost never when I'm alone. But one special occasion was the day I opened a package from Dink Flamingo, stretched out on the couch, hit the remote, and watched *Out of the Brig*.

And noticed I had missed a spot when I cleaned the monitor.

☆13☆ Navy Daze

Anonymous

All American, seventeen, high school graduate, and now enlisted in the Navy—that was me. I never dreamed that when I returned I would be as bisexual as a honey bee! One fine spring day in 1944 I entered Camp Farragut, in Idaho, for boot camp training. It was not long before I went off, or up, like a skyrocket! At that time I must have been somewhat of a sweetie pie, just ready to be eaten. I did have an innocent baby face, gold hair, and, strangely enough, *brown* eyes. However, for size and weight I was as rough and tough as any of the older fellows, and stronger than many of them. All I needed was training . . . and the gay old Navy soon gave me that! But it was different training from what anyone would expect.

It is hard to comprehend my bashfulness then. The farther away from the older groups I could stay the happier I was. I liked to be alone, and I made excuses to wash and rewash my clothes in order to be by myself. I attended religious services on Sunday for the feeling of safety. During drill I would tensely force myself to march in step so as not to be left on the field after everyone else was gone. I was actually afraid of the instructor who was in charge of me. At night when the barracks was sleeping and I was safe in bed, I was often so overcome with homesickness that I felt like bawling. I should have uttered a peep or two, and I probably wouldn't have been so damn lonesome!

It was about then that my first fantastic experience took place. One thing should be made clear, however. I was not innocent as to *sex*. I can remember sticking my ding-dong into the neighbor girls. This never seemed to harm me any, and I was always as hot as a blast furnace. Just the slightest touch or rub of my cock and it would get stiff. It seems as though half of my childhood was spent with a hard-on. Most of the time in school classrooms I had one. I know if it ever got soft I would wiggle my legs and get it hot again. I liked that muscle hard all the time. I can remember the wildly thrilling sensations I would get when I went off. They used to leave me trembling and weak, they were so violent. When I was in the fifth or sixth grade, there was one hot little girl named Caroline who lived nearby and was simply nuts for my organ. I almost fucked her to death. That's a fact; she became so skinny and nervous that her mother was constantly and frantically giving her tonics and medicines to build her up. All this time I was busy wearing her down. I recall many times when our folks were away, we would climb all over the davenport fucking in every possible position. I can still visualize my prod slipping in and out of her, and she would squeal and jerk about until she was almost in hysterics from the pleasure of it.

My cock was not responsible for Caroline's skinniness, however, because I had no ill effects. In fact all this practice only seemed to make me hotter, and the exercise must have made my prod bigger, although it was a good size even then. I never stopped marveling at how it could swell up so big and round, and get so burning hot. Caroline's favorite sport was playing in the attic of her home, or ours. I'll bet a cherry she played with herself many times, and she took on other boys too when I was not available. In the attic she used to get me on top of a pile of blankets that was covered by an old padded comforter as my mother called it. We would play house until I was pooped to a frazzle.

In those days I could only go off twice, or at the most three tricks. Then she would be after me to stick my fingers in her for half an hour or until I got disgusted and wanted to do something else. Caroline grew up to be a real bitch and finally married some dumb cluck who didn't know anything but fucking.

There was another thing that had a bearing on my life in the Navy and should be mentioned. I always had plenty of exercise, especially swimming, almost every day in the summer. My father had a farm where I rode horseback a lot and could meet the neighboring farm girls. I soon found out that they liked to screw just as much as the city girls and actually knew more about it from watching the farm-yard love affairs. On the farm, I experimented with a sheep, as well as a heifer, and one time let a calf suck me off. These interludes did not intrigue me much, as there was enough two-legged stuff around to keep me occupied. We lived in town, where my father had a second-hand store that sold about everything. It was there I met a lot of rather wild soldiers from a nearby Army camp. Often they would be rather high on a half-gallon of California wine and, when my father was not close by, would tell me amazing tales about big-city whore-houses and Chinese girls who had slits sideways.

At Camp Farragut all the new recruits received several types of shots and then were ready for rough exercise, including swimming practice. This was a snap for me, and I began to lose some of my bash-fulness. We were told to try and make it around the pool as many times as we could. I kept on for what seemed like a couple of hours, long after everyone else had quit, and was finally told to get out. Later they classed me as the leading swimmer of the base. Up until that time I had not tried swimming in bed!

The company commander said that I could be of great use to him at the pool, working as the instructor. I reported the next morning. God, I used to hate some of those bats from Midwest states, who had never seen water in such a compact form as swimming pools. When it came to actually floating in the stuff they did not know whether they were going up or down, and I couldn't tell either.

Instructions went on after the regular classes had left the pool. I tried never to have more than two in the water with me at once. In fact, giving all my attention to one swimmer seemed to soothe him and give him confidence. Often a farm boy would get upset when I grabbed him around his nude waist, for instance to teach him how to kick the correct way. Many of these fellows would blush standing nude in front of me and try to hide their dong with their hands. After a few days of this sort of exposure they soon learned that we were all born with the same things between our legs. Sexologists are certainly on the ball when they say that confinement of any kind can change anyone. Put a hot young lad in a barracks or aboard ship without a single thing to occupy his mind, and you can be sure he will soon be beating his meat or playing off with his buddy. Unless he is by nature very cold. Laying in my rack those first few nights, waiting for reveille to blow, I learned what the groaning and squeaking of the beds meant. However, with high-powered Navy rules, this innocent offense is enough to bring you a discharge.

The head of the barracks, incidentally, is the natural meeting place for those who like to show off or need to expose themselves to others during the act of a hand job. I have seen a lot of fellows put on a race to see who could come first . . . and some of them could sure come.

Anyway, one night I was teaching a giant Texas kid the art of swimming across the pool without sinking to the bottom, and it appeared that I was getting nowhere fast. We were alone in the building, and I secretly wished that bastard would drown so that I could go to bed.

"Okay, Mac, come here," I told him. "Goddamn it to hell, kick your feet like I told you to. Here, I'll show you one more time." My hand reached for his hips so I could help hold him up, in an effort to make him really swim. His nude body brushed against mine. A strange feeling raced up and down my spine. It was as though an electric shock had passed through our bodies. This powerful kid gave me one of his dreamy smiles. The next thing I knew his arms slipped about me and we were pressed close together.

"I am tired as hell of this swimming," he murmured. "Let's you and me do something else."

Suddenly his hot full lips were clinging to mine, and I could feel his hard velvety body against mine and his huge organ pressing up against my leg.

I didn't know what to do . . . and I didn't much care. Finally we just stood there, chest deep in the warm water, and looked at each other. I said without much enthusiasm, "Knock it off, mate. I've got enough work to do without this kind of fucking."

"Hell, you want to get your gun off," he remarked. "You are just as hot as I am. I know, 'cause you didn't resist. Let's go to a locker room or somewhere."

I was ready for anything he had to offer, and he led the way. We found a room that had a bed and locked the door.

"Could I brown you?" he asked.

"With that mast you've got? Christ, no," I told him. "Are you nuts?"

"You can't with me," he said. "To tell the truth, I don't know how. I've never tried that."

The big bastard was even more bashful than me. I was about to tell him that there was nothing to it, when he continued, "I guess we could try a blow if you're game. How about that? A sixty-nine?"

I dried myself off and lay down on the bed. "Go to it," I told him. I already had a bursting hard-on from just thinking about the matter.

He started in giving me a real tongue job, and the suction soon had me feeling so wonderful I could have done anything for him, but I didn't, although his huge nude body was sprawled there beside me. I wanted to find out what the score really was with him. I had heard of some butch guys who would do a sixty-nine or about anything else, and then run off as loose as a goose. Almost before they could get the come wiped off their mouths, they would be blabbing to their so-called normal pals that "a queer put the make on me." Mr. Butch would say, "Why, Christ! This friggin' Navy!"

With my mind in a fog, I thought I was dreaming as this fellow kept on with his sucking. The hot, slippery feeling on my tool was sure getting me aroused. At last, I grabbed hold of his mighty shaft with my hand and massaged it. That powerful muscle seemed to expand even more the moment I touched it, and began throbbing and quivering as if it would explode. I was just about to reach a climax myself and my other hand slipped down to my love pole, but with the power of a weight lifter he pushed it away and continued his devastating play. "Faster," I cried, but he insisted on making this passion bout a slow affair. He sure knew his love methods, and that there is far greater thrill in delaying the action.

Finally I could hold off no longer and began twisting about in a frenzy. Then he really clamped his mouth down and brought me to a terrific spasm of the most glorious ecstasy. He didn't take my load in his mouth, however, but pressed the pumping muscle down against my belly. I was covered with a flood of my own cream.

Apparently my lover was burning hot himself. He switched around and buried his head beside mine. His powerful arm held me flat and I was spread-eagle on the bed, my legs forced wide apart by his heavier ones. I could feel his implement pressing and moving across my warm belly. He began to moan with delight; I knew it wouldn't take him too long to work himself off against my body. The very thought of lying naked on top of another warm body gets me aroused. Now he was rubbing his face against mine and his tongue was caressing my ear. The pressure of his weight on my joy stick, and his big burning one brushing against it every so often had me going again too. I realized I would reach another climax very shortly.

It was as though an earthquake was beginning. I could feel his body quiver on top of me, and the tense muscles. His cannon began to throb and shoot great blasts of hot sticky lust liquid, until it had pumped all over my chest clear up to my tits. That was too much for me. I let go and started going off too. I couldn't describe the thrills and emotions that engulfed me. I had never been so overcome with wild, passionate pleasure.

Later, we just lay there, exhausted, gazing into each other's eyes. At last he grinned and asked, "What's your name?"

I told him. "What in the hell's yours?"

"Bill," he answered. "Goll-ee, we about had a time."

"Texas, Bill, eh?" I remarked. "Well, you're a damned old bastard. Getting me all covered with lather."

After we had showered and dressed, he said, "I'll be over for another swimming lesson tomorrow night, if you'll be here."

"I'll be here all right, mate," I assured him, "with balls on, and looking down the drag for you."

I slept better that night than I had in a long, long time.

After that we became regular pals and went almost everywhere together. He was a nice guy, and we had loads of fun, especially when he came for his extra swimming lessons. After he got sent to a ship, I was lonely as the devil for a while. However, there were different guys after me all through boot training. My chances for more experiences of this type were many, but I thought no one else in the wide world could compare with Bill. There were about seventy-five fellows in our barracks, and at night I often heard guys slipping in and out of other guys' sacks.

There was one big scandal at Farragut, and about twenty fellows got booted out. They had formed a regular fuck club and would go to Spokane, where they would rent hotel rooms, and had some rare times. It got so they would even entertain a lot of their buddies, picking up any innocent, hard-up fellow and initiating him into what can be accomplished in a hotel room. Often he would be taken from room to room, no doubt trying out the various beds until he was milked dry. One of them finally picked up an officer who was a prick and made a stink about the affair, and everybody got their butts hauled on the carpet.

The next thing that happened to me, after completing the training at Farragut, occurred after I was sent to a battleship that was tied up and waiting for a crew at Bremerton, Washington. There was an officer named Burkhardt who taught recognition aboard ship. He had been a lawyer with the Standard Oil company in private life before getting his commission, and he could surely size a fellow up. He picked me out of the seventy-eight in his division to be his assistant. He just walked up to me and asked how I would like to work for him. Afraid to say no, I consented. There was nothing feminine about him, but I soon found out that he was a perfect auntie. He once told me that he had his wife lay on top of him when they fucked.

Lieutenant Burkhardt didn't waste any time. Late the very next afternoon in his office we had a frank little discussion . . . that ended up with him giving me a blow. He got so hot over this that he went off. I did too, of course, but didn't enjoy it much as I was so surprised. It turned out that I was blessed with this kind of service as long as I was under his protective wing.

The next main thing that happened to me at Bremerton was entirely different. Being only seventeen and looking it, I discovered that it was difficult to find excitement when on liberty. One evening I walked the streets alone but finally got up enough nerve to enter a bar and order a beer. There was an awful lot of sailors in the place, all having a loud time. To my surprise I was served without any questions asked, even though I must have stood out like a jackrabbit among wolves.

I was downing my second brew when I felt a hand on my shoulder. "If it isn't doll face," said a big good-looking sailor. "Where have you been keeping yourself? Come on over to our table and have one."

I had never seen the guy before in my life. At his table there were five other guys guzzling and gabbing. When they saw me, one asked my new companion, "Where'd you find the chicken?" Another remarked, "Save me some." Then one of them asked me, "Kiddo, do you go for sea-pussy?"

I had no idea what in the hell they were talking about. I had no more than got seated when one of the younger fellows poured a shot of whiskey into my glass of beer. Not realizing what the outcome would be, I swilled it down. Before very long I was feeling a little light-headed. I began to act as rough as I could and became very friendly with all of my drinking partners.

They kept talking about the "Spinning Wheel," and finally I asked what that was.*

"Great God, baby, have you never been there?" exclaimed one. "It's a nightclub over in Seattle where they have female impersonators. You can meet *everybody* there."

To me it seemed like these big husky sailors were talking rather bitchy, but I hadn't heard anything yet. Soon we were joined by another guy they all knew, who was accused of being too potted to speak clearly.

"Damn my broken bridgework!" exclaimed the new arrival, waving his hand. "Mary! Didn't I ever tell you about my living with that old son-of-a-bitch Dr. Erdhart for three years? Why, one day he laid a thousand dollars on the table and told me it was mine if I would have my front teeth pulled and bridgework put in. He thought the

*The Spinning Wheel is mentioned on the first page of Don Paulson's book *An Evening at the Garden of Allah: A Gay Cabaret in Seattle* (New York: Columbia University Press, 1996). See also Gary L. Atkins, *Gay Seattle: Stories of Exile and Belonging* (Seattle: University of Washington Press, 2003).

sensation would be wonderful then. Well, honey, I did, but, girls, it was weeks before I could even open my mouth far enough to go around a *pencil,* and he had a piece of meat you could wrap around your neck three times and tie a bow! Oh! This bitch Navy calling. . . . When I went up for my physical, I told the physician I was as queer as rosewater. 'So what?' he said. 'Keep your legs crossed. But how about a date tonight?' He *said* that to me! Really my dears, I thought I'd flop on the floor! 'Keep your legs crossed,' he said. . . ." With that, Uncle Sam's fighting seaman fell into hysterical laughter and couldn't stop.

"Oh, the silly crappy slut," said the young sailor near me. "I swear she's told us that story a dozen times." He dumped another slug of whiskey into my beer.

After three or four more of those boilermakers, my head seemed to be moving around quite detached from my body. At last I let it rest on the shoulder of the big blond fellow who had brought me over to the table. I was nine sheets to the wind but I could still realize what was taking place. For the life of me, I could feel a hand traveling up and down the pant leg of my tailor-mades.

"Are you sleepy, fella?" murmured my new friend.

"Yeah, I'd better crawl back to the ship."

He said to the others, "This one wants to go home." They started talking about going home.

Home? I began to think about it and felt awfully forlorn. The next thing I knew, of all times, I had to go on a crying jag.

"Take it easy, boy," he said. "This is Saturday night! Stay in town with me. I have a room just down the street."

"Let's go now," I said. "I feel . . . awful dizzy."

That was it, as I remember. We got up to leave. He placed his huge arm around my waist and, with my head on his shoulder and another of his buddies at my back, I was ushered to his lair.

When we entered the room, they put me to bed, and while one held me the other undressed me. Then they stripped also. There was a small light on a table by the bed. My pal, the blond guy, turned me over on my stomach. Then he was on top of me like a cat pouncing on a mouse.

The fool's drunk, I thought.

But he wasn't that drunk. He reached over to his shaving kit on the little table and got a jar of cold cream. I knew now. I began to gurgle and protest.

"Shut up, you cute little chicken," he purred in my ear. "I won't hurt you, just relax."

How could I relax with this big bum on top of me? I commenced to struggle, but he spread my legs apart with his hands, while his partner helped hold me down.

"No . . . no," I said.

"Yes, yes," he said and began kissing my neck.

I guess that did it. . . . I was too high to resist him anymore. Even though that damned dong of his looked to me about the size of an electric light pole. He started shoving it in, and it hurt. But after it was in it didn't hurt anymore . . . just felt funny . . . and I relaxed some. He began working it in and out, and each time I would flinch, he would pause and take it easy. After that a change came over me. My own joy stick had swelled up under me, pressing against the soft bed, and was beginning to feel good. Pleasant, lustful sensation slowly gripped my whole body, spreading and growing more intense as he worked faster. I didn't mind this at all anymore. In fact, I began to stretch out and move in unison with his plunging thrusts. My loins were on fire now from the pressure and excitement. The feeling nearly drove me frantic. I began moaning. My pal was murmuring words in my ears.

His friend who had held my arms down now let go. He couldn't stand to watch the act any longer. I got a good look at him at last as he stood beside the bed. He was built about like myself. A little heavier, and more wiry, with a lot of dark hair on his chest. This was the fellow who had poured me all the shots of whiskey. Well, bless his damn queer soul, it would be his turn next. I hadn't thought of that. These guys were too fresh, raping me like this. They had a lot of nerve, the bastards. But what the hell.

Dark hair was doing something now. . . . He pulled the pillow away and got on the bed. Sitting down, he lifted my head up, so his legs were under my shoulders. Christ, that long dark dong of his was right in front of my nose. Slowly, his hands slipped around my neck, forcing my head down. His legs began to move, pressing forward. I didn't give a damn anymore. I sucked on him then . . . like a baby who hadn't had a tittie in days.

"Oh God," he whispered.

I was getting it from both ways—and I was building up to a climax. I was going to explode, but I managed to hold off for a moment.

"You fucking bastards," I choked, "I'm going off." My giant lover on top moved slightly to one side and from somewhere he produced a towel and shoved it under me.

"You are doing swell, kid. Don't mess up the sheet, or you'll have to sleep in it."

He started in again. The guy in front of me was leaning forward. Glancing up I saw that the blond was kissing the dark-haired one. What a deal. I was on the home stretch at last . . . in a whirl of uncontrollable pleasure. The blond was having a spasm, and the one in front was in a fit of ecstasy too. A last passionate lunge into my buttocks, then I could feel warm liquid running down over my balls. Just about then my mouth was filled with shooting spurt. Cream was pouring into me from both ends, and I was shooting it out at the same time. I lost track of everything then. . . .

We untangled ourselves and lay there exhausted. Later, I cuddled up to the blond, my head against his chest. I drifted toward sleep and was content.

About the Editor

Alex Buchman is a former United States Marine. He served during the Gulf War and was honorably discharged. His first book, *A Night in the Barracks: Authentic Accounts of Sex in the Armed Forces* (Haworth) topped the *Washington Blade* best-seller list based on gay and independent bookstore sales nationwide; was nominated by Susie Bright for inclusion in her *Best American Erotica* series; and was praised by the respected *San Francisco Bay Guardian* for "an emotional charge of a strength and vividness all but unknown in the fancier, more pretentious precincts of same-sex fiction." Buchman lives in San Diego, California.

Contributors

Dink Flamingo is the man behind <ActiveDuty.com>. Since 1996 he has "shot close to 100 videos" and has "been close to 700 men"—most all of them soldiers. "Barracks Bad Boys & Samurai Sally" is his first work to appear in print.

Steve Kokker's credits include two other Russian military tales in, respectively, Alex Buchman's *A Night in the Barracks* (Haworth, 2001) and Steven Zeeland's *Military Trade* (Haworth, 1999). He has also directed the films *Happiness Is Just a Thing Called Joe* (Canada, 1998), a tribute to Joe Dallesandro, and *Komrades* (Canada/Russia, 2003), about life in the Russian military ("Charming!"–*Variety*). Otherwise, he writes travel books for Lonely Planet and lives most of the time in Tallinn, Estonia. His permanent e-mail address is <maadlus@ infonet.ee>.

Daniel Luckenbill was drafted into the U.S. Army in 1967. He attended Officer Candidate School, was commissioned 2nd Lieutenant, Field Artillery, and served in Vietnam (1968-1969). He studied writing under Christopher Isherwood, John Rechy, Elisabeth Nonas, and Terry Wolverton. His many publishing credits include "Ask a Marine," anthologized in Ian Young's *On the Line: New Gay Fiction* (Crossing Press, 1981). Luckenbill's memoir of Isherwood is featured in the Lambda Literary Award winning *The Isherwood Century* (Wisconsin, 2000), and his story "Tomorrow's Man" appeared in *A Night in the Barracks*. He is secretary of the Board of Directors, ONE Institute and Archives, Los Angeles. He is currently working on additional stories and a novel about his military experiences in Vietnam. He lives in Hollywood and Twentynine Palms, California.

This is **Gayle Martin's** second published story. Her first, "Barracks Gang Bang," appeared in *A Night in the Barracks*. She lives in LA. When she's not picking up Marines in Oceanside she's mourning the devaluation of her laserdisc collection and completing a memoir of her years working in the sex industry.

Steven Zeeland is the author of *Barrack Buddies and Soldier Lovers* (Haworth, 1992), *Sailors and Sexual Identity* (1994), *The Masculine Marine* (1996), and *Military Trade* (1999). His private correspondence with Mark Simpson, published as *The Queen Is Dead: Jarheads, Eggheads, Serial Killers & Bad Sex* (London: Arcadia, 2001), was ranked one of the year's best books by *The Independent on Sunday*. A Spanish language edition is forthcoming from Océano de México. Zeeland's photographs of Navy men have been published in *Attitude, Dutch, Honcho,* and *The Village Voice*. He has directed a "porn" video called *Out of the Brig* and a related short film, *Joe the Sailor*. His official Web site is <www.stevenzeeland.com>.

Order a copy of this book with this form or online at:
http://www.haworthpress.com/store/product.asp?sku=5094

BARRACKS BAD BOYS
Authentic Accounts of Sex in the Armed Forces

_______in softbound at $12.95 (ISBN: 1-56023-367-2)

Or order online and use special offer code HEC25 in the shopping cart.

COST OF BOOKS________

POSTAGE & HANDLING________
(US: $4.00 for first book & $1.50 for each additional book)
(Outside US: $5.00 for first book & $2.00 for each additional book)

SUBTOTAL________

IN CANADA: ADD 7% GST________

STATE TAX________
(NY, OH, MN, CA, IL, IN, & SD residents, add appropriate local sales tax)

FINAL TOTAL________
(If paying in Canadian funds, convert using the current exchange rate, UNESCO coupons welcome)

☐ **BILL ME LATER:** (Bill-me option is good on US/Canada/Mexico orders only; not good to jobbers, wholesalers, or subscription agencies.)

☐ Check here if billing address is different from shipping address and attach purchase order and billing address information.

Signature________________________

☐ **PAYMENT ENCLOSED:** $________________

☐ **PLEASE CHARGE TO MY CREDIT CARD.**

☐ Visa ☐ MasterCard ☐ AmEx ☐ Discover ☐ Diner's Club ☐ Eurocard ☐ JCB

Account # ________________________

Exp. Date________________________

Signature________________________

Prices in US dollars and subject to change without notice.

NAME________________________

INSTITUTION________________________

ADDRESS________________________

CITY________________________

STATE/ZIP________________________

COUNTRY________________ COUNTY (NY residents only)________________

TEL________________ FAX________________

E-MAIL________________________

May we use your e-mail address for confirmations and other types of information? ☐ Yes ☐ No We appreciate receiving your e-mail address and fax number. Haworth would like to e-mail or fax special discount offers to you, as a preferred customer. **We will never share, rent, or exchange your e-mail address or fax number.** We regard such actions as an invasion of your privacy.

Order From Your Local Bookstore or Directly From

The Haworth Press, Inc.

10 Alice Street, Binghamton, New York 13904-1580 • USA
TELEPHONE: 1-800-HAWORTH (1-800-429-6784) / Outside US/Canada: (607) 722-5857
FAX: 1-800-895-0582 / Outside US/Canada: (607) 771-0012
E-mailto: orders@haworthpress.com

For orders outside US and Canada, you may wish to order through your local sales representative, distributor, or bookseller.
For information, see http://haworthpress.com/distributors

(Discounts are available for individual orders in US and Canada only, not booksellers/distributors.)

PLEASE PHOTOCOPY THIS FORM FOR YOUR PERSONAL USE.

http://www.HaworthPress.com BOF04